The Crossroads

JESUS
LOVES YOU
MINISTRIES

Compliments of

The King's Kettle
Food Pantry
30 N. Fayette St.
Shippensburg, PA 17257

SELECTED FICTION WORKS BY L. RON HUBBARD

FANTASY

The Case of the Friendly Corpse
Death's Deputy
Fear
The Ghoul
The Indigestible Triton
Slaves of Sleep & The Masters of Sleep
Typewriter in the Sky
The Ultimate Adventure

SCIENCE FICTION

Battlefield Earth
The Conquest of Space
The End Is Not Yet
Final Blackout
The Kilkenny Cats
The Kingslayer
The Mission Earth Dekalogy*
Ole Doc Methuselah
To the Stars

ADVENTURE

The Hell Job series

WESTERN

Buckskin Brigades
Empty Saddles
Guns of Mark Jardine
Hot Lead Payoff

A full list of L. Ron Hubbard's
novellas and short stories is provided at the back.

*Dekalogy—a group of ten volumes

L. RON HUBBARD

The Crossroads

GALAXY PRESS

Published by
Galaxy Press, LLC
7051 Hollywood Boulevard, Suite 200
Hollywood, CA 90028

Printed in the United States of America.

ISBN-10 1-59212-368-6
ISBN-13 978-1-59212-368-1

Library of Congress Control Number: 2007928019

Contents

Stories from Pulp Fiction's Golden Age

A ND it *was* a golden age. The 1930s and 1940s were a vibrant, seminal time for a gigantic audience of eager readers, probably the largest per capita audience of readers in American history. The magazine racks were chock-full of publications with ragged trims, garish cover art, cheap brown pulp paper, low cover prices—and the most excitement you could hold in your hands.

"Pulp" magazines, named for their rough-cut, pulpwood paper, were a vehicle for more amazing tales than Scheherazade could have told in a million and one nights. Set apart from higher-class "slick" magazines, printed on fancy glossy paper with quality artwork and superior production values, the pulps were for the "rest of us," adventure story after adventure story for people who liked to *read*. Pulp fiction authors were no-holds-barred entertainers—real storytellers. They were more interested in a thrilling plot twist, a horrific villain or a white-knuckle adventure than they were in lavish prose or convoluted metaphors.

The sheer volume of tales released during this wondrous golden age remains unmatched in any other period of literary history—hundreds of thousands of published stories in over nine hundred different magazines. Some titles lasted only an issue or two; many magazines succumbed to paper shortages during World War II, while others endured for decades yet. Pulp fiction remains as a treasure trove of stories you can read, stories you can love, stories you can remember. The stories were driven by plot and character, with grand heroes, terrible villains, beautiful damsels (often in distress), diabolical plots, amazing places, breathless romances. The readers wanted to be taken beyond the mundane, to live adventures far removed from their ordinary lives—and the pulps rarely failed to deliver.

In that regard, pulp fiction stands in the tradition of all memorable literature. For as history has shown, good stories are much more than fancy prose. William Shakespeare, Charles Dickens, Jules Verne, Alexandre Dumas—many of the greatest literary figures wrote their fiction for the readers, not simply literary colleagues and academic admirers. And writers for pulp magazines were no exception. These publications reached an audience that dwarfed the circulations of today's short story magazines. Issues of the pulps were scooped up and read by over thirty million avid readers each month.

Because pulp fiction writers were often paid no more than a cent a word, they had to become prolific or starve. They also had to write aggressively. As Richard Kyle, publisher and editor of *Argosy*, the first and most long-lived of the pulps, so pointedly explained: "The pulp magazine writers, the best of them, worked for markets that did not write for critics or attempt to satisfy timid advertisers. Not having to answer to anyone other than their readers, they wrote about human beings on the edges of the unknown, in those new lands the future would explore. They wrote for what we would become, not for what we had already been."

Some of the more lasting names that graced the pulps include H. P. Lovecraft, Edgar Rice Burroughs, Robert E. Howard, Max Brand, Louis L'Amour, Elmore Leonard, Dashiell Hammett, Raymond Chandler, Erle Stanley Gardner, John D. MacDonald, Ray Bradbury, Isaac Asimov, Robert Heinlein—and, of course, L. Ron Hubbard.

In a word, he was among the most prolific and popular writers of the era. He was also the most enduring—hence this series—and certainly among the most legendary. It all began only months after he first tried his hand at fiction, with L. Ron Hubbard tales appearing in *Thrilling Adventures, Argosy, Five-Novels Monthly, Detective Fiction Weekly, Top-Notch, Texas Ranger, War Birds, Western Stories,* even *Romantic Range.* He could write on any subject, in any genre, from jungle explorers to deep-sea divers, from G-men and gangsters, cowboys and flying aces to mountain climbers, hard-boiled detectives and spies. But he really began to shine when he turned his talent to science fiction and fantasy of which he authored nearly fifty novels or novelettes to forever change the shape of those genres.

Following in the tradition of such famed authors as Herman Melville, Mark Twain, Jack London and Ernest Hemingway, Ron Hubbard actually lived adventures that his own characters would have admired—as an ethnologist among primitive tribes, as prospector and engineer in hostile climes, as a captain of vessels on four oceans. He even wrote a series of articles for *Argosy,* called "Hell Job," in which he lived and told of the most dangerous professions a man could put his hand to.

Finally, and just for good measure, he was also an accomplished photographer, artist, filmmaker, musician and educator. But he was first and foremost a *writer,* and that's the L. Ron Hubbard we come to know through the pages of this volume.

This library of Stories from the Golden Age presents the best of L. Ron Hubbard's fiction from the heyday of storytelling, the Golden Age of the pulp magazines. In these eighty volumes, readers are treated to a full banquet of 153 stories, a kaleidoscope of tales representing every imaginable genre: science fiction, fantasy, western, mystery, thriller, horror, even romance—action of all kinds and in all places.

Because the pulps themselves were printed on such inexpensive paper with high acid content, issues were not meant to endure. As the years go by, the original issues of every pulp from *Argosy* through *Zeppelin Stories* continue crumbling into brittle, brown dust. This library preserves the L. Ron Hubbard tales from that era, presented with a distinctive look that brings back the nostalgic flavor of those times.

L. Ron Hubbard's Stories from the Golden Age has something for every taste, every reader. These tales will return you to a time when fiction was good clean entertainment and the most fun a kid could have on a rainy afternoon or the best thing an adult could enjoy after a long day at work. Pick up a volume, and remember what reading is supposed to be all about. Remember curling up with a *great story.*

—Kevin J. Anderson

KEVIN J. ANDERSON *is the author of more than ninety critically acclaimed works of speculative fiction, including* The Saga of Seven Suns, *the continuation of the* Dune Chronicles *with Brian Herbert, and his* New York Times *bestselling novelization of L. Ron Hubbard's* Ai! Pedrito!

The Crossroads

The Crossroads

I T was not like Eben Smith to resign himself to the fates and vagaries of an economic muddle he could not fathom, not even to the AAA or the HOLC or the FLC or the other various unsyllabic combinations which he regularly, each morning, collected in his RFD box.

"It ain't right," he said that dawn to Maria his wife and Lucy his horse. "I can grow crops and I know crops and there ain't nobody in Jefferson County that can grow more corn per acre and what's more better corn per stalk than me. And when it comes to turnips and squash and leaf lettuce I reckon I ain't so far behind. And by cracky there must be some place where the stuff can be sold so folks can eat."

"The guvvermunt paid you right smart for all that plowing under you did, Eben," cautioned his wife.

"Well I reckon I don't give a spit how smart they paid me because it all went out in taxes so they could pay me agin. No sir, Maria," and here he had to pause and grunt while he made Lucy take the bit, "it ain't right. Them city papers when they ain't atalking about some furriner fightin' some other furriner is saying how people is starving in the streets. Well, I can't figure it out. Here I'm the best corn raiser in Jefferson County and I got lots of corn . . . and squash and turnips and leaf lettuce too, by gum . . . and still the guvvermunt says I got to stop raisin' what I planted and plow under what I was goin' to plant. It's like that guvvermunt man said yesterday when I asked him what the dingdong it was all about, the economic problems is acute. And by golly our economic problems is going to get even more acute if we don't get some hams and things for this winter. Like my grandfather Boswell that traded a spavined mare for the purtiest prize bull in Ohio used to say, 'Politics is a subjeck for men that's got full bellies . . . otherwise it ain't politics, it's war.' We ain't no paupers that we got to be supported by no charity and if they's folks starvin' in the city, why, I reckon they got somethin' or other to trade for turnips and truck."

"Now, Eben," said Maria, anxiously wiping her hands on her apron, "don't you go doin' nothin' to get the guvvermunt mad with you. Mebbe this thing you're goin' to do ain't got any place in this here economic system acuteness."

"Never did hear anythin' wrong with a man fillin' his belly so long as he didn't have to steal to do it," said Eben, picking up the lines and trailing them to the box seat of the spring wagon.

"Mebbe them city folks'll trade you right out'n everything and you'll have to walk home," protested Maria as she worriedly swept an unruly strand of gray hair from her tired eyes.

"Listen at the woman!" said the offended Eben to Lucy the mare. "Maria, I reckon as how you're forgettin' that time I swapped a belt buckle for one of them newfangled double-action hand-lever self-draining washing machines for you. Giddap, Lucy."

The heavily sagging wagon finally decided to follow along on the hoofs of Lucy and while Maria held open the gate, creaked out into the ruts of the dirt road. Eben's hunting setter came leaping excitedly after, having been awakened in the nick of time by the noisy wheels.

"Git for home, Boozer!" said Eben severely.

Mystified, the dog stopped, took a few hesitant steps after the wagon and then, seeing Eben shake his whip as a warning, halted, one foot raised, eyes miserable, tail drooping, to stand there staring after, while the spring wagon's yellow dust got further and further away, smaller and smaller until it vanished over a slight roll in the limitless prairie.

Eben looked like a simile for determination. His lean, wind-burned, plow-hardened, tobacco-stained, overalled, shrewd-eyed self might have served as a model for a modern painter in the need of a typical New Englander type peculiar to the Middle West. But Eben was not quite as sure as he appeared. What Maria had said about the city folks had shaken him. Dagnab women anyhow. Always makin' a man feel uncertain of hisself! Wasn't he Vermont stock? Hadn't his folks, in Vermont, England, China and Iowa, to say nothing of the Fiji Isles and Ohio, bargained and businessed everybody in sight out of their shirts? Yankee traders or the direct descendants of them were just plain impossible to trim unless it was by each other. Still . . . he'd never been away from this expanse of green and yellow prairie and, no matter his own folks, he wasn't sure. Things had changed out in the world. Mebbe them stores in the city wasn't as easy to deal with as Jeb Hawkins' down at Corn Center. He looked with misgivings at his wagonload. Under the tarp were turnips and lettuce and corn and some early apples, making the canvas cover bulge. They were tangibles. With his own hands he had brought them into strength in this world and by golly there weren't turnips or lettuce or corn like that anywhere else in Jefferson County.

Plow them under?

If folks was starving then by golly they needed food. That was simple. And if they had anything at all Eben knew he could bring whatever it was back and trade it to Johnny Bach or Jim Johnson or George Thompson. They had all the lettuce and apples and corn and turnips they needed and they had hams and a lot of other truck Eben needed. And Jeb Hawkins' store would trade him whatever else . . . Surely it was a simple transaction.

He began to maunder on what things he might get for his produce and how he would convert them and how he would go about trading for them or something else and so passed the hours of the morning.

Because he lived down at the south end of Jefferson County and had always traveled north to Corn Center, he was not sure of his road nor, indeed, sure of his destination. People spoke of the city and pointed south and that was little enough to go upon. Twice he paused and asked directions, getting vague replies, and drove on until noon. Lucy nuzzled her feed bag and Eben ate the lunch Maria had prepared and then sat half an hour under a tree beside a brook wondering indistinctly on his project.

Through the better portion of the afternoon he continued on southward. The country became more level and less inhabited and he began to be homesick. His eyes did not like looking for ten miles to a flat horizon without so much as a poplar, a ditch or a rolling hill to ease the sameness. He was even less sure of himself than he had been at noon. He'd spend the night beside the road, a fact which did not worry him, and he couldn't starve with a load of vegetables. But if this city was many days away, why, Lucy would run plumb out of grain and he didn't like to think of how she'd begin to look at him if she had to eat nothing but dusty grass.

Dusk came and then darkness and Eben, disliking to stop because he might yet see the city in the distance, continued onward, wrapping a sheepskin around his feet to keep them warm.

When the stars said it was about eight and when Eben was about to give up for the night, he came to a crossroads.

"Whoa," he said to Lucy. And then looked about him.

Here four roads made an intersection and so irregular was their departure from this spot and so widely different was their quality that Eben was very perplexed. One road was concrete or at least white and hard like that one the WPA had put down through Corn Center. The road to the right of that, going away from Eben, was full of large green-gray boulders and seemed nearly impassable to anything except foot traffic. The next was hard and shiny and metallic and threw back the stars so that, at first, Eben thought it was wet. Then, of course, there was his own, a double rut worn

7

into twin prisons for narrow wheels and baked there by the September sun.

Eben got down and felt of each one, appreciative of the quality of the shiny metal one except that a horse would probably fall down on it the first rain. The white, hard one wasn't quite like that road in Corn Center because it was dusty, besides it showed the tracks of horses but no wheels and that one in Corn Center showed nothing. Although he had been certain that the country was all flat, the boulder-strewn way came down a hill to this place and, crossing it, ran up a hill and vanished.

Then an oddity struck Eben. For the past few minutes that he had been on this intersection the sun had been at high noon! He put his thumb in his eye and peered at it accusingly and then because it was quite definitely the sun and obviously there, he shook his head and muttered:

"Never can tell what the goldurned guvvermunt is going to do next!"

Lucy was eyeing him forlornly and he forgot about the sun to remember that she was probably hungry and that he was nearly starved himself. He hung the feedbag on her nose and, making her move the wagon so that it was not on any of the right of ways, took out the remains of the lunch Maria had fixed and munched philosophically with the warm sun on his back. He felt drowsy after that and, stretching out, slept.

He did not know how long he had been lying there for when he awoke the sun was still at high noon.

"Wilt the whole lot!" he grumbled, spreading the canvas

more tightly and thoroughly over his load. He hunted around until he found a spring among the boulders and, after watering Lucy, sluiced the canvas.

Methodically, then, he took up the problem of the roads. One of these must lead to the city but with four from which to choose he rapidly became groggy with indecision. He sat down in the wagon's shadow and waited for somebody to come along with information.

The hours drifted by though the sun did not move and Eben was nearly upon the point of continuing along his own dirt track when he saw something moving among the rocks up the hill. He got up and hailed and the something moved cautiously down toward him, from boulder to boulder.

The newcomer was a bearded old fellow in a greasy brown robe which was his only covering. Bits of tallow and sod clung in his gray whiskers and a hunted look lurked in his watery eyes.

"Long live the Messiah!" said the old man.

"What Messiah?" said Eben, offended at the vigor if the old man meant what he thought he meant.

"Long live Byles the Messiah!" said the old man.

"Never heard of him," said Eben.

The old man stared in amazement and then slowly began to examine Eben from toe to straw hat, shaking his head doubtfully.

"You aren't like anyone I ever saw before," said the old man. "From whence dost thou come?"

"Jefferson County," said Eben.

"It must be far, far away," said the old man. "I have never heard of it. Are you telling the truth when you say you have never heard of Byles, the Messiah?"

"Yep," said Eben. "And what's more I don't reckon I care whether I hear about him or not. I want to know which road to take to get to the city."

The old man looked around. "I have never been along any of these roads. In fact, I don't remember this crossroad at all no matter how many times I have come down this hill. And as for a city, why I know only of Gloryville and Halleluyah, one behind me and one before me on this road I travel."

"I never heard of either of them," said Eben. "But I got to find out which one goes to the city because I've got a load of vegetables here that I aim to trade to the city folk."

"Vegetables! At this season of the year?"

"Why not? It's September, ain't it?"

"September! Why thou must be mad. This is January!"

Eben shrugged. "That ain't finding the way to the city."

"Wait," said the old man. "See here. You say you have vegetables. Let me see them."

Eben lifted the edge of the canvas and the old man began to gloat and his jaws to slaver. He picked up a turnip and marveled over it. He caressed a leaf of lettuce. He stroked the rosy skin of an apple. And when he picked up a beautiful ear of corn he cooed.

Eben was a trader. His eye became shrewd and his pose indolent. "I reckon the wagon's pretty heavy anyway. If mebbe you got something or other to trade I might let you have somethin'. 'Course vegetables—in January—is pretty scarce and the city folks will be willin' to pay a right smart amount. But mebbe now you got somethin' valuable that might persuade me to trade. I ain't asayin' I will but I ain't asayin' I won't."

"Wait here!" cried the old man and bounded up the hill as though mounted on springs.

Eben waited for an hour with patience, pondering what article the old man might produce for trade. It was certain he couldn't have much for he seemed very thin and poor.

There was a tinkling of donkey bells and, in a moment, half a dozen men leading beasts of burden came into sight and down the hill. Eben had misgivings. He was sure he had not any use whatever for six donkeys. But the donkeys were not the articles of trade. The men brought the animals to a halt and unloaded from them with ceremony two big jugs a beast.

"Now!" said the old man. "These for your wagonload of vegetables."

Eben looked dubious. He plucked a shoot of grass and chewed it. "Can't say as I'm much enthused."

"Not . . . not enthused! Why, by the saints! My good fellow, these jars be full of the famous Glory Monastery Brandy!"

"Reckon I ain't got no license to sell liquor," said Eben.

"But it's all we have!" cried the old man. "And we are starved for good food! The peasants have to spend so much time praying during the summer that they hardly get a chance to plant and so we have to make them fast all winter. Only this brandy, made from grapes grown on our slopes, is in abundance." He stepped nearer Eben, whispering. "It's Byles' favorite brandy and that's why we make so much of it."

"Nope," said Eben.

"But just taste it!" cried the old man.

"Don't drink," said Eben. "I reckon I better be getting on to the city."

"Please don't leave!" begged the old man. "Carlos! Run back and bring up *twelve* donkey loads of brandy."

Carlos and the others hurried away and Eben philosophically chewed his shoot of grass until they came back and the additional twenty-four jars were unloaded.

"Now," begged the old man. "Will you trade?"

It came to Eben that many of his vegetables might possibly spoil if he kept them until he reached the city and of course he might be able to do something about the brandy.

"Well . . ." said Eben. "I might give you a few things. This brandy is pretty cheap in the city."

"How much will you give us?"

"Well . . . mebbe a quarter of the load. After all you only got thirty-six jars here and they hold mebbe not more than five gallons apiece and . . ." he scratched with his toe in the dirt, ". . . that's only about a hundred and eighty gallons of brandy. Yep, I can let you have a quarter of the load—providing you let me do the selecting."

They agreed and presently the mules were laden with turnips and corn and leaf lettuce and apples and the wagon was lighter by a quarter.

Eben watched them pick their way among the rocks, up

the hill and out of sight until their voices, badly mixed in a dolorous hymn about one Byles, faded to nothing.

He then began to lift the brandy off the road and into the wagon. But he very soon found, to the tune of a snapping spring, that he had made far too good a trade. Not only was he unable to transport this stuff but unless he lightened his vegetable load he could not go on with this injured wagon. Scowling he started to walk up the hill to see if he could find a sapling with which to mend his wagon. But he did not get far from the wagon before the thump of marching feet brought him hurrying back.

Sixteen soldiers, with an officer, were coming along the dusty white road. They formed two files between which marched five men whose heads were bowed and whose hands were tied. Eben was not familiar with the dull-gray of their uniforms but he suspected that maybe the guvvermunt had changed the color since he'd last seen army men. Soldiers, officer and prisoners paid him no attention but marched on along the white road and around the edge of a chalky cliff and out of sight. Shortly after there was a blast of firing followed by four more blasts and the soldiers with their officer came marching back.

Business concluded, the officer saw Eben. At the leader's signal the column of men stopped and their dust behind them settled. The officer stared at Eben, then at the wagon, then at Lucy and back to the wagon. Finally his eye lingered upon the jars.

"Who are you and what are you doing here?" demanded the officer.

"I'm Eben Smith and I reckon the guvvermunt would be plumb put out if anything was to happen to me."

"Put out?" and the officer laughed loudly. "My man, I suppose you do not realize that a totalitarian state is far too powerful to be overthrown. You have seen what happens to the enemies of the Greater Dictatorship. What do you have there?"

"Brandy," said Eben.

"What?"

"Brandy and vegetables."

"And what, may I ask, is brandy?"

"You drink it," said Eben.

"Hmmm," said the officer. "I must inspect this."

Eben got a water bucket out of his wagon and poured a couple gallons of brandy into it. He handed the bucket to the officer who drank thirstily.

It surprised Eben that the fellow did not choke or gasp and then he realized that this brandy must be of a very smooth quality indeed. The officer handed the bucket on to his men. It was soon empty.

"Fill it up," said the officer.

About half an hour later the officer and the soldiers were sitting in a semicircle around the tail of the wagon, telling one another they were all the best of friends.

"Fill it up wunsh more," said the officer.

Eben filled up the bucket but he did not present it. "Who," he said, "is going to pay for this? Brandy is very expensive."

"Charge it to the state," said the officer. And then thought better of it and reached into his pocket, bringing out a roll of paper. He tendered a bill. "That'sh plenty to pay for it. Now give me the bucket."

Eben shook his head. "This must be Confederate money like my grandfather Boswell used to talk about. It won't pay for the brandy."

"Sergeant!" bawled the officer. "Arrest thish man for treashon!"

But when the sergeant got up he promptly fell flat on his ugly face and when the soldiers got up they fell down.

"Maybe you could take something elsh for payment," said the officer.

Eben had been wishing for some time that he was not there all alone at the mercies of these soldiers. And now he looked at them shrewdly. "Well, I reckon mebbe I might take a few rifles."

"What?"

"Well," said Eben, "this brandy is pretty expensive. And if you don't pay me for it and leave me alone why I don't guess I'll be able to get any more of it for you. Mebbe I can trade some of these rifles to Jeb Hawkins for rabbit hunting."

"Can't do it," said the officer.

"No more brandy," said Eben.

Three hours later the last soldier had wobbled away and sixteen rifles, sixteen bullet bandoliers, one automatic and five clips lay under the canvas along with the vegetables. Once more Eben searched for a sapling to bond his broken spring for he was certain now that he would not abandon so much as a drop of the remaining hundred and seventy gallons of brandy.

As soon as he got to the top of the boulder-strewn hill, it became dark and he could not find any trees. As soon as he walked around the cliff on the white road and found the graves there he abandoned that section. He was just about to explore the metal road when something was seen to be moving along it. Eben went back to his wagon and waited.

It was the strangest kind of a vehicle he had ever seen for it had no wheels. It was just a big, gleaming box which scudded along the surface without a sound. There was something frightening about it.

When it came abreast of the wagon it stopped and a section of it clanked outward. A thing which was possibly a man, leaned out, staring at Eben. Its head was nearly as big as its body and it had two antennae waving above its brow as well as its huge, pupilless eyes.

"Musta escaped from some carnival," muttered Eben to himself.

"ERTADU BITSY NUSTERD HUABWD UDF IUWUS KSUBA NADR," said the driver.

"Reckon you must be some furriner," said Eben. "I don't understand you."

"RTFD HRGA BJBKUT BTSFRD KTYFTY?" said the driver.

"Can't you talk English?" said Eben curiously.

The driver got out. His spindly legs did not lift him to a height in excess of Eben's shirt pocket. He began to rummage around inside the cab of the wheelless vehicle and finally produced some tubes and coils which he assembled rapidly into some sort of instrument. This he plugged into a hole in the side of the vehicle and then aimed a sort of megaphone at Eben.

"RTDR UTDF BJYSTS JIRFTC GYTFCV HUBJYT?" said the driver.

"That's a funny-looking outfit you got there," said Eben. "But shucks, I seen a lot of radios that was better. The thing don't even play."

The driver twiddled the dials while Eben spoke and then, much mystified, left off. "BRSD TYRT RTFDAY!"

"Don't do no good," said Eben. "I can't understand a word of it."

On that the driver beamed. He tuned one dial sharply. "Then you speak elementary English," said the phone.

"Of course I do. And if you do too, why didn't you do so in the first place?"

"I think you will not be insulted if I do. But usually, you know, it is considered vulgar to talk plain English. Tell me, can't you really encipher?"

"Don't reckon I ever caught myself doing it," said Eben, amused.

The driver walked around Eben, examining him. "In our language schools, you know," said the phone, "we encipher and decipher as we speak. It is grammatically correct. But you seem to be from some very distant land where plain English is still spoken. It must be a very dull place."

"I reckon we get along," said Eben. "What you got in that thing, there?"

17

"The truck? Oh, some junk. I was taking it down to the city dump. What have you got in that thing?"

"Well," said Eben, "I got some brandy and I got some vegetables but they're both pretty valuable."

"Brandy? Vegetables? I don't know those two words."

Eben chuckled to himself. And this feller was accusing *him* of being ignorant! "Well, I'll show you."

He gave the fellow an apple and the driver immediately pulled a small lens of a peculiar color from his pocket and looked it all over.

"It's to eat," said Eben.

"Eat?" blinked the driver, antennae waving in alarm.

"Sure," said Eben.

More anxiously than before the driver remade his examination. "Well, there's no poison in it," he said doubtfully. And then he bit it with his puny teeth and presently smiled. "Why, that is very good indeed! RTDA HRTA—"

"Now don't start that again," said Eben.

"It's excellent," said the driver. "Do you have many of these?"

"They're pretty rare," said Eben.

"What is that in the jars?"

Eben gave him a drink of the brandy and again the driver beamed.

"How this warms one! It's marvelous! Could I buy some from you?" And he took out a card which had holes punched in it.

"What's this?" said Eben.

"That's a labor card, of course. It shows my value. Of course as the driver of a waste wagon I don't earn very much, only forty labor units a week, but it should be sufficient—"

*"Well," said Eben, "I got some brandy and I got
some vegetables but they're both pretty valuable."
"Brandy? Vegetables? I don't know those two words."*

"What kind of junk have you got in that wagon?"

"What does that have to do with my buying some of this?" said the driver.

"Mebbe we can cook up a trade," said Eben.

"Trade? What is trade?"

"Well, you got something I might want and I got something you want and so we swap. I give you what I got and you give me what you got and there you are."

"How quaint! Never heard of such a thing. But I haven't anything in my truck that you could want."

"Never can tell," said Eben.

The driver lifted up the top of the box vehicle and Eben, peering in, very nearly fell in!

The whole load was gold bracelets and necklaces and diamond and ruby rings!

Eben could not trust his speech for a little while and then, casually, "That looks like gold." He tossed a bracelet indolently in his horny hand, feeling its weight.

"Yes, of course," said the driver.

"Real gold."

"Certainly," said the driver.

"Reckon," said Eben, eyeing the other with shrewdness, "you figure this ain't much account."

"Well, since transmutation factories lowered the price on gold to three units a ton nobody wants to wear it and the Street Department had to clean up the back of the Woman's Distribution Center and so I am taking it down to the city dump of course. It is much easier to make sand into gold than to remelt the gold."

"Then I reckon this load is worth, at three a ton, mebbe six-seven dollars. Tell you what I'll do. I'll give you a basket of apples and a jar of brandy for the lot."

The driver looked at Eben in astonishment and then, before the man could change his mind, leaped into the truck and backed it swiftly to eject the load of jewelry beside the spring wagon. Sweatingly he then lifted the five gallon jar of brandy and the basket of apples into his cab and went scudding back from whence he had come without another word.

Eben felt uncomfortable. Very seldom did his conscience bother him about a trade, but now . . . He picked up pieces of jewelry at random and bit them, leaving clear teeth dents in them. It most certainly was gold!

Immediately upon that he became even more uncomfortable. Supposing somebody came along and stole it! Hurriedly he began to carry it behind a bush and bury it and as he worked another alarming thought came to him. People would think he'd stolen it! He should have gotten a bill of sale! And as he did not have one he would never dare let on that he had this stuff. Forlornly he finished hiding it. Why, they'd send him to jail for years and years! They'd say he'd gone and robbed somebody! And then came the final blow! The guvvermunt said it was against the law to have gold! He'd broken the law! And they'd put him away for years and years!

"Hullo!"

He leaped about to find that his preoccupation had let four men in uniform come up the chalky road unnoticed. They had a very severe appearance but still there was a furtiveness about them which belied instant aggressiveness.

21

"A little while ago," said the spokesman, a young man, "a friend of ours came along here and got something from you."

"Wasn't my fault," said Eben.

"No, no, you don't understand. He and his soldiers came back singing and walking in circles and muttering about a wonderful drink and . . . well . . . we became curious, naturally, as to what made them so happy."

Eben looked them over. "Well . . . I guess it won't do no harm. It was brandy. There's some of it in the water bucket."

The spokesman drank and smacked his lips. He passed the bucket to his companions and they drank ecstatically, handing the empty bucket back for replenishment.

"Nope," said Eben.

"Sir, we are officers in the Hurricane Guard of the Dictator himself!"

"That don't make no difference," said Eben. "If you want brandy you got to trade me something for it."

They studied him for a while and then went into conference among themselves. Then they again consulted Eben.

"We will buy your brandy," said the eager young spokesman. "How much do you want for it?" And he offered the assembled capital of the four.

"Money's no good," said Eben. "It's got to be a swap."

They again went into a huddle and then the spokesman said, "We haven't anything to swap you except guns. There aren't anything but guns in our whole country because when we conquered everybody there was nobody left to produce anything except guns."

"Well . . ." said Eben doubtfully, "guns ain't worth much."

"But you'll take them?"

"Well . . ."

The four officers were gone in a flurry of chalk dust.

Eben sat down on a boulder beside his wagon and watched Lucy crop grass now that she was released from harness. The gold worried him and these officers worried him for he could not quite understand why they really would trade. If they had guns it seemed more likely that they use them to take what they wanted. Perhaps, though, they didn't want to disclose the source of the brandy or cut off its supply. Still, if they found this gold they wouldn't bargain about that. They'd just take it without so much as giving him a blessing. Eben went over to see how the gold was getting along and was engaged in covering up some of it that could be seen to glitter. It grieved him that he had to abandon it, it was so pretty. The most he could take would be some necklaces and bracelets for Maria.

While so engaged he was again accosted and at the sound of the hail he turned to find the soldiers coming back. Hastily he got away from the gold and then, seeing what was arriving, momentarily forgot about it.

He had said guns and now, it seemed, he was getting guns! In a long procession he saw soldiers dragging at wheeled machine guns and ammunition carts and light antitank rifles and their caissons. Soldiers, soldiers, soldiers and guns, guns, guns. And each soldier had a furtive look about him.

The young officer who had made the bargain was evidently

a businessman beneath his rank stripes. "Sir," he said, "we are bringing you guns. All these guns for all that brandy. We offer the trade and if you refuse it, we offer the guns another way."

Eben stared at the arsenal which was mounting up beside his wagon, towering and then towering again until the pyramid was spilling arms into the road. He wanted to say no but the sign of this force got the better of his judgment. He made no protest when the brandy was carted away, all hundred and seventy gallons of it. The memory of the five dead prisoners was strong upon him. And so the brandy and the soldiers were soon vanished, leaving Eben with enough materials for a good-sized war. He tried to be hopeful. But he was certain, the longer he sat looking at that pile of weapons, that he had been bested. What good were machine guns against rabbits? And there were only rabbits in Jefferson County. Why, all he knew about the things was what young Tom Stebbins had said when he came back from the marines.

Dolorously he took one of the long barrels and mounted it upon its tripod. And then, being a Yankee, his mechanical spirit was stirred by the mystery of it. The thing was so complicated that it challenged his ingenuity. He finally found how to pull back the loading handle and then, going from there, figured out the way to put a belt through the loading slot. The result far exceeded his expectations. With a shattering roar bullets flung out from the weapon and carved a long trench in the hill. He let go of the trigger and blinked at the thing. Little by little he pieced together the way it worked and so engrossed did he become that he was startled when the old man from the Glory Monastery put a hand on his shoulder.

"Wh—oh, hello," said Eben.

The old man was staring in fascination at the machine gun. "What manner of instrument is that?"

"It's a machine gun," said Eben.

The old man looked at the mighty pile of them. "But you have so many!"

"Enough to start a war," said Eben.

"War?"

"Well, that's what they use these for," said Eben. And wishing to show off his newly acquired skill he sent a ferocious burst into the hill. Rocks and dust flew violently.

"Do . . . do they all act like that?" said the old man.

"Yep," said Eben. And he showed him how to load and fire it. The old man got up from the tripod shaking, but evidently not from fear.

"You wait here," said the old man and then, with beard and cassock flowing behind, streamed up the hill and out of sight. He was gone for nearly two hours and Eben began to think that he had been scared away and was just beginning to swear at himself for not having traded off some more vegetables when the old man came streaming back, followed closely by several monks.

"Now do that again," said the old man.

"What?"

"Shoot that thing."

Eben loaded and fired it and the newcomers tch-tched as they watched the dirt fly out of the hill.

"Are they all alike?" said the old man.

"Well, some of them are bigger," said Eben.

"Let's see how they work," said the old man.

Eben wheeled out an antitank rifle and, after thinking it over for a few minutes, got it loaded and fired. The shell blew a great gouge from the hill and lifted a boulder ten feet in the air.

"You see?" said the old man to his friends.

"We see," they said grimly.

"And?" said the old man.

"You are right," said his friends.

"Bring the donkeys," said the old man.

At a signal, nearly a hundred donkeys came tinkling over the hill, each one loaded with two five gallon jugs of brandy.

"Wait a minute," said Eben. "You want to trade that for these guns?"

"Certainly," said the old man. "We're sick of shouting 'Long Live Byles' from morning until night. Besides we don't think he's the Messiah. We're almost certain that I am."

"Well," said Eben, chewing thoughtfully on a shoot of grass, "these here machine guns and cannons come pretty high. Now you got just about enough there to buy three of them."

"Thr-Three?" said the old man.

"The ammunition, of course," said Eben, "is extra."

The old man looked at the guns and then at the long line of donkeys. He sighed and then, glancing at the gouged hill, brightened. "All right. Men, unload and go back for more."

Some four hours later there were no more guns anywhere

in sight. But nearly a half-acre of ground was covered by stone jars. Eben walked thoughtfully between the wide rows, lifting a cover here and there and smelling the stuff.

It was better, far better, to have brandy, though he did not know exactly why. It was something tangible and, unlike guns or gold, was not likely to get him into trouble. Of course he would have to figure out a way to transport all this and a way to sell it. . . .

With a swoosh, the rectangular box slid to a halt beside the spring wagon. Lucy looked inquiringly at it and then went on champing her grass.

"ERTDBRDTD!" said the driver.

"Hello," said Eben, walking over and putting his elbow on the window.

"I came back about those apples," said the driver.

"Yep?" said Eben.

"I brought another truck load of gold for a basket of them."

Eben swiftly shook his head. "Nope."

"You mean you won't trade like you did?"

"Nope."

"Say, you can't do that! Why . . . why, I sold those apples for a labor unit apiece and I've got buyers until I can't count them. You can't refuse!"

"Nope," said Eben. "No trade."

The driver pushed out of the truck. "Not even one basket? Not just one? This is much better gold. I got it off the dump north of town. It's in bars!"

"Nope," said Eben.

The driver pointed to the brandy. "You don't have to give

me one of those. That made everybody sick. So you are getting a better bargain than ever. Only half of what you gave me before! And twice as much weight in gold!"

"Nope," said Eben.

The antennae waved in disgust and the driver leaped into the other end of his wheelless truck and swooshed away from there, without even saying goodbye.

Eben sighed deeply. It pained him to have to refuse such a trade. But if the guvvermunt said that having gold was agin the law, then it was agin the law. He'd already put his neck in the noose for having a couple tons of it. . . .

There was a steady tramp nearby and Eben whirled to see that the white road was thick with soldiers and guns! They were marching without regard to order and each one was eagerly towing some sort of weapon and some had, among them, a big piece of artillery and its caissons. The air was thick with the dust of their coming and the road about Eben was thick with clamoring men.

"We want some of that stuff," said a junior officer, thrusting a submachine gun at Eben. He had evidently already had a drink from his luckier mates, just enough to stimulate his desire for more.

"Nope," said Eben. "That brandy—"

"We offer a trade and if we don't get what we came for," growled the officer, "then we'll take it anyway! We are the regimental guard of Lomano the Lurid himself and what we do we do and what we want we want. Now is it a trade?"

Eben sat down dejectedly and watched his brandy vanish

jar by jar up the long chalk road. And some time later he dolorously inspected a park of miscellaneous weapons and ammunition. Business was not so good, he decided, for it was not likely that there could be much more brandy at the Glory Monastery. Well . . . he still had his vegetables. And ten baskets of apples. Maybe he'd better get out of here while he possessed that much negotiable capital.

SWOOSH! SWOOSH! SWOOSH! SWOOSH! SWOOSH! SWOOSH! SWOOSH! SWOOSH!

Truck after wheelless truck came to a stop on the metal road and driver after driver, big-headed and spindle-legged, jumped out to surround Eben.

"Now," said the driver who had already been there. "Do we trade or don't we trade? This is my union and in each one of these trucks is a full load of gold."

"I reckon I have to be sorry," said Eben, "but—"

There was a whirr and a crackle as of a leaping arc and the world grew dim for Eben. He caught at his wagon and slumped down, wholly unconscious.

It was, of course, still high noon when he woke up. The trucks were gone. The vegetables and apples were gone.

Eben sighed, staring into the empty spring wagon. He was thankful to at least show no mark of what they had done to him save for a slight headache. The robbers!

And then he turned and saw that in some twenty places at the rate of two tons or more a place the trucks had dumped their contents. Gold! Gold, gold, gold, gold, gold, gold, gold! And more gold! ! ! ! ! !

"Oh . . . ," groaned Eben. There must be forty or fifty tons of it!

Gold, gold, gold, gold . . .

"Hullo!"

Eben nodded wearily to the old man. And then, noticing that he was powder-stained and high with excitement, took interest.

"More guns," said the old man. "He's got the United Order of Fanatics against us! We've got to have more guns and more ammunition!"

Eben waved a tired hand toward the wide park of guns.

"Ah!" cried the old man ecstatically. "And as for the trade, our credit will have to be good. We have brandy but no time to transport it."

"Brandy in hand," said Eben, reviving, "or no guns!"

There was a shattering roar up on the hill and Eben ducked from the swarm of singing slugs which barely missed his head.

"Is our credit good?" demanded the old man.

"Sure!" said Eben.

And then the park was emptied by half a hundred toiling, battle-stained monks and Eben's capital went rolling over the boulders and out of sight up the hill.

He sank down upon a boulder. His capital was gone save for this accursed gold. And if the guvvermunt found all this gold around him they'd put him away for years if not as a thief then at least as a horder. Life became bitter to Eben. He was hungry. Lucy was out of grain. His wagon was empty and he had nothing negotiable unless it was gold, a commodity which would surely get him into a great deal of trouble.

It could not be worse. He had better abandon the wagon and ride Lucy back home.

He had made this decision and was in the act of whistling for Lucy when he saw a knot of men come hurrying down the chalk road toward him. They stopped, threw themselves down and fired with their rifles at something Eben could not see. Then they leaped up and sped swiftly toward him.

A gray-headed, corpse-faced giant was in the lead. His muchly-braided uniform was torn and his hat was gone and his sword scabbard was empty. He almost rushed by Eben and then came to an abrupt halt, glaring. The few soldiers with him clustered about.

"Is this the devil?" said the giant.

"Probably," said a soldier.

"Did you or did you not sell brandy to my bodyguard in return for their guns?" snarled the giant.

"Well—" said Eben.

"So it is true! It is true that I, Lomano the Lurid, am revolted against because of you, you miserable lout! Colcha! Shoot this man!"

"Your Dictatorship, there isn't much time. The people are hard on our heels!"

"Shoot him! He has cost me my realms!" roared Lomano.

But just as Colcha raised his rifle there was a burst of firing from down the chalk road and the soldiers dropped down and fired swiftly back, driving their pursuers to cover. Then, once more Colcha started to do his duty.

"You, the trader!" hailed a voice. And Eben was almost happy to see the old man and an armed bodyguard come rushing down the hill.

"What's this?" said Lomano.

Then the chalk road's distance belched more bullets and Lomano and his troops decided they had tarried too long. Not knowing the intentions of the old man and his group, they dashed off and around the cliff and out of sight. A moment later a stream of indifferently armed peasants loped up the chalk road and rounded the chalk cliff in pursuit of Lomano.

Eben sighed with relief and was ready to express his thanks to the old man when that worthy came up, panting and glaring.

"You, the trader!" said the old man. "Have you any more guns?"

"No," said Eben swiftly, "but if you pay me what you owe me I can possibly get you as many more as you want."

"Hah! I thought so. What use have I for guns now that I have won! And you would sell them to another who would oppose me. Sir, you find before you the Messiah! And you who threatens my existence must be disposed of here and now!"

"Hey!" said Eben. "You owe me money. You took my guns and you owe me—"

"Sir, if you have any last prayers, say them."

"Wait a minute," begged Eben. "You can't do this. If you say you don't want me to sell guns then just pay me what you owe me and I'll be on my way and never come back—"

"Sir, this cannot be. I, the Messiah after Byles (God rest his soul), command that this menace to my rule be removed!"

SWOOSH! SWOOSH! SWOOSH!

Three wheelless cars, not dissimilar to the trucks save that they had windows instead of blank sides, rushed up to a halt on the metal road. Out of them poured a swarm of big-eyed men with antennae.

The new Messiah gaped at the weird beings and his men, in alarm, fell back. The beings swarmed around Eben and the Messiah took to his heels with his crew.

"BN FRDH HYST MAHG?" said an officer to the driver Eben had first seen.

"FRYST," said the driver, quivering.

The officer fished into his metal shirt and pulled out a sheet with dots on it. He looked at Eben and then at the paper.

"I understand that you speak vulgar English. Therefore I shall decipher this order as I go. Attend!

'Whereas the strange being at the Crossroads delivered into the hands of one CARTD various articles to be known as HYSTFA and FACRT and whereas one CARTD did disseminate to the populace of FEJAUG said HYSTFA and FACRT and whereas the populace of FEJAUG does now clamor for fresh and bulky food against the wise counsel of the GAUANFT PYHSTRA that food pills are far superior thus upsetting the public order, it is hereby discovered that there has been a sag in the time tracks and that appropriate steps must be taken to rectify the error.

'Signed
'HAYCST'"

Thereupon the workmen, with magnetic slings, whisked blasters out of their cars and made holes. After this they produced a dozen weighty hydraulic jacks which soon had their heads thrusting against the boulder-strewn road. Up, up, up went the road and then, abruptly, vanished.

Next they attacked the problem of the chalk road, working efficiently and without a sound. Up, up, up went the chalk road and then faded into nothingness.

The jacks were shifted and more holes blasted. And then the workmen had purchase on the metal road and, with them on it, it began to rise. Up, up, up!

Eben leaped for the edge and landed with a jar upon his own world's dirt track. Overhead the metal strip continued to lift and then, with a puff, it was no longer to be seen.

Lucy raised her head from cropping grass and looked thoughtfully at Eben. She gave a startled grunt as some clods of dirt dropped out of the clear sky and something sparkled as it hit her on the nose. She looked pained.

Dejectedly Eben dragged her over to the spring wagon and hitched her up. He sat for a while looking upward and then, with a shake of his head which designated complete abandonment of the whole thing, he went over to where Lucy had been standing and picked up the diamond ring and two ruby bracelets which had fallen out of the bottom of the hole in which he had buried them.

The next morning Eben drove into his yard and was instantly almost devoured by an ecstatic Boozer. The dog leaped down out of the wagon and ran in circles, emitting glad yelps which noise set the whole barnyard into an uproar.

"Mercy sakes," said Maria, coming to the door. "What . . . OH! EBEN!" And she raced to him as he was getting down and threw her arms about him, beginning to cry.

He pried her off, not ungently. "Here, here. No need to cry. I got home didn't I?"

"Oh, Eben!" she wept. "I am so glad to see you! Five whole months and no word from you—"

"Five months!"

"Yes, five months! Oh, Eben, I th-thought you were d-d-d-ead!"

Eben looked about and saw for the first time that the fresh green of spring and not the dying green of fall was in the fields.

"Good gosh!" said Eben. "And without any plowing done!"

"I just knew something dreadful was going to happen when you left. What *did* happen?"

"I traded off my vegetables," said Eben. He put the ring and the bracelets in her hand. "These are for you. Now get me some dinner and let me get at this plowing. Good gosh! March and no plowing done!"

Borrowed Glory

Borrowed Glory

HUMAN beings," said Tuffaron, familiarly known as the Mad Genie, "are stupid and willful. They derive intense enjoyment from suffering or else they would not bend all their efforts toward suffering."

He sat back upon the hot rock this hotter day and gazed off into the dun wilderness, stroking his fang to give himself an air of contemplation and wisdom.

Georgie bustled her wings with resentment. Her lower lip protruded and her usually angelic countenance darkened. "Know-it-all!" she taunted. "Conceited know-it-all!"

"That is no way for an angel to talk, Georgie," said Tuffaron.

"Conceited, bloated know-it-all!" she cried and then and there felt a growing desire to kick his huge column of a leg. Of course she wouldn't, for that would not be exactly an expression of love for everything. "Prove it!" she demanded.

"Why," said Tuffaron, the Mad Genie, in his most lofty tone, "human beings prove it themselves."

"You evade me. You are the stupid one!" said Georgie. "I dare you to put that matter to test. Human beings are very nice, very, very nice and I love them. So there!"

"You are under orders to love everything, even human beings," said Tuffaron. "And why should I exert myself to labor a point already too beautifully established?"

"Coward!" said Georgie.

Tuffaron looked down at her and thoughtfully considered her virginal whiteness, the graceful slope of her wings, the pink of her tiny toes showing from beneath her radiant gown. "Georgie, I would not try to trifle with such proof if I were you. Besides, you have nothing to wager."

"I am not allowed to wager."

"See?" said Tuffaron. "You are afraid to prove your own point, for you know quite well you cannot."

"I'll wager my magic ring against your magic snuffbox that I can prove you wrong," said Georgie.

"Ah," said Tuffaron. "But how do you propose to prove this?"

"The outer limit of my power is to grant anything for forty-eight hours."

"Certainly, but according to the law, if you grant anything for forty-eight hours you have to have it back in forty-eight hours."

"Just so. A human being," declared Georgie, "is so starved for comfort and happiness that if he is granted all for just a short time he will be content."

"My dear, you do not know humans."

"Is it a wager?"

"A sure thing is never a wager," said Tuffaron, "but I will place my magic snuffbox against your magic ring that if you give all for forty-eight hours you will only succeed in creating misery. My precept is well known."

"The wager is stated. I shall grant all for forty-eight hours and even though I must take it back at the end of the time, I shall succeed in leaving happiness."

Solemnly he wrapped his huge black hand about her dainty little white one. She eyed him defiantly as they sealed the bargain. And then she leaped up and flew swiftly away.

Tuffaron barked a guffaw. "I have always wanted an angel ring," he told the hot day.

It was not warm in the room and one might have kept butter on the ancient radiator. A trickle of bitter wind came in under the door, gulped what warmth there was to be found in the place and then with a triumphant swoop went soaring up and out through the cracked pane at the window's top.

It was not warm but it was clean, this room. Patient hands had polished the floor with much scrubbing; the walls of the room bore erasure marks but no spots of smudge. The tiny kitchenette might not have a quarter in its gas meter but it had bright red paper edging its shelves and the scanty utensils were burnished into mirrors; the tea towels, though ragged, were newly washed and even the dishcloth was white—but this last was more because there had been nothing with which to soil dishes for many days. A half loaf of bread and a chunk of very cheap cheese stood in solitary bravery upon the cupboard shelf.

The little, worn lady who napped upon the bed was not unlike the shawl which covered her—a lovely weave but tattered edges and thin warp and a bleach which comes with time.

Meredith Smith's little hand, outflung against the pillow, matched the whiteness of the case save where the veins showed blue. It was a hand which reminded one of a doll's.

She slept. To her, as years went on, sleep was more and more the only thing left for her to do. It was as though an exhausting life had robbed her of rest, so that now when she no longer had work to do she could at least make up lost sleep.

From the age of eighteen to the age of sixty she had been a stenographer in the Hayward Life Co. She had written billions of words in letters for them. She had kept the files of her department in neat and exact order. She would have had a pension now but Hayward Life was a defunct organization and had been so for the past six years.

Relief brought Meredith Smith enough for her rent and a small allowance of food but she was not officious and demanding enough to extract from the authorities a sufficiency.

But she did not mind poverty. She did not mind cold. There was only one sharp pain with her now and one which she felt was a pain which should be accepted, endured. It had come about three years ago when she had chanced to read a poem in which old age was paid by its memory of love and it had swept over her like a blinding flood that she, Meredith Smith, had no payment for that age. The only thing she had saved was a decent burial, two hundred and twenty dollars beneath the rug.

She had worked. There had been many women who had married out of work. But she had worked. She had been neither beautiful nor ugly. She had merely been efficient. At times she had thought to herself that on some future day she must find, at last, that thing for which her heart was starved. But it had always been a future day and now, at sixty-six, there would never be one.

She had never loved a man. She had never been loved by a child. She had had a long succession of efficient days where her typewriter had clattered busily and loudly as though to muffle her lack.

She had never had anyone. She had been a small soul in a great city, scarcely knowing who worked at the next desk. And so it had been; from eighteen to sixty. And now . . .

It was easier now to sleep and try not to think of it. For she would die without having once known affection, jealousy, ecstasy or true pain.

She had been useless. She had run a typewriter. She had been nothing to life. She had never known beauty; she had never known laughter; she had never known pain; and she would die without ever having lived, she would die without a single tear to fall upon her going. She had never been known, to be forgotten. Yesterdays reached back in a long gray chain like pages written with a single word and without punctuation. Tomorrow stretched out gray; gray and then black. A long, long time black. And she was forgotten before she was gone and she had nothing to forget except emptiness.

But the hand which touched her hand so warmly did not startle her and it did not seem strange for her faded blue eyes to open upon a lovely girl. The door had been locked but Meredith Smith did not think of that, for this visitor was sitting upon the edge of the bed and smiling at her so calmly and pleasantly that one could never think of her as an intruder.

"You are Meredith Smith?" said the visitor.

The old lady smiled. "What is your name?"

"I am called Georgette, Meredith. Do not be afraid."

"I am glad you came."

"Thank you. You see very few people, I think."

"No one," said Meredith, "except the relief agent each week."

"Meredith Smith, would you like to see people?"

"I don't understand you."

"Meredith Smith, would you like to see people and be young again and dance and laugh and be in love?"

The old lady's eyes became moist. She smiled, afraid to be eager.

"Would you like to do these things, Meredith Smith, if only for forty-eight hours, knowing that you would again come here and be old?"

"For forty-eight hours—to be young, to dance, to laugh, to be in love—even if only for forty-eight hours." She was still afraid and spoke very quietly.

"Then," said Georgie, "I tell you now," and she had a small stick with a glowing thing upon its end, "that for forty-eight hours, beginning this minute, you can have everything for which you ask and everything done which you want done. But you must know that at the end of the forty-eight hours, everything for which you ask will be taken back."

"Yes," said Meredith in a whisper. "Oh, yes!"

"It is now eight o'clock in the morning," said Georgie. "At eight AM day after tomorrow, all things I gave you will have to be returned, save only memory. But until then, Meredith Smith, all things you want are yours."

It did not particularly surprise Meredith that her visitor did not go away as a normal person should but dissolved,

"Then," said Georgie, "I tell you now," and she had a small stick with a glowing thing upon its end, "that for forty-eight hours, beginning this minute, you can have everything for which you ask and everything done which you want done."

glowed and vanished. Meredith sat looking at the imprint on the bed where Georgette had been seated. And then Meredith rose.

YOUTH! BEAUTY!

In her mirror she watched and her fluttering heart began to grow stronger and stronger. Her hair turned from gray to soft, burnished chestnut. Her eyes grew larger and longer and brightened into a blue which was deep and lovely and warm. Her skin became fresh and pink and radiant. She smiled at herself and her beautiful mouth bowed open to reveal sparkling, even teeth. There came a taut, breath-catching curve in her throat and the unseen hand which molded her flowed over her form, rounding it, giving it grace, giving it allure and poise—

YOUTH!

A gay darling of eighteen stared with lip-parted wonder at herself.

BEAUTY!

Ah, beauty!

She was not able to longer retain the somber rags of her clothes and with a prodigal hand ripped them away and, naked, held out her arms and waltzed airily about the room, thrilled to the edge of tears but laughing instead.

"Meredith, Meredith," she said to the mirror, posed as she halted. "Meredith, Meredith," she said again, intrigued by the warm charm of the new voice which came softly and throbbingly out of herself.

Ah, yes, a young beauty. A proud young beauty who could

yet be tender and yielding, whose laughter was gay and told of passion and love—

"Meredith, Meredith," she whispered and kissed herself in the mirror.

Where were those dead years? Gone and done. Where were those lightless days? Cut through now by the brilliance of this vision she beheld. Where was the heartache of never having belonged or suffered? Gone, gone. All gone now. For everything might be taken back but this memory, and the memory, that would be enough! Forty-eight hours. And already those hours were speeding.

What to wear? She did not even know enough of current styles to ask properly. And then she solved it with a giggle at her own brightness.

"I wish for a morning outfit of the most enhancing and modern style possible."

CLOTHES!

They rustled upon the furniture and lay still, new in expensive boxes. A saucy little hat. Sheer stockings so thrilling to the touch. A white linen dress with a piqué collar and a small bolero to match. Long white gloves smooth to the cheek. And underthings. And graceful shoes.

She dressed, lingering ecstatically over the process, enjoying the touch of the fabrics, reveling in the new clean smell of silk and leather.

She enjoyed herself in the glass, turning and turning back, posing and turning again. And then she drew on the gloves, picked up the purse and stepped out of her room.

She was not seen in the hall or on the stairs. She wrinkled a pert little nose at the sordid street.

"A car," she said. "A wonderful car, very long and smooth to ride in, and a haughty chauffeur and footman to drive it."

"Your car, *mademoiselle*," said the stiffly standing footman, six feet tall and his chin resting on a cloud.

For a moment she was awed by his austerity and she nearly drew back as though he could look through her and know that it was a masquerade. But she did not want him to see how daunted she was and so she stepped into the limousine. Still frightened she settled back upon the white leather upholstery.

"The . . . ah, the park—James."

"Very good, *mademoiselle*." And the footman stepped into the front seat and said to the chauffeur, "*Mademoiselle* requires to ride in the park."

They hummed away and up the street and through the town and soon they were spinning between the green acres of Central Park, one of a flowing line of traffic. She was aware of people who stopped and glanced toward her, for it was a lovely car and in it she knew they saw a lovely girl. She felt suddenly unhappy and conspicuous. And it worried her that the chauffeur and footman knew that this was a masquerade.

"Stop," she said into the phone.

The car drew up beside a curbed walk and she got out.

"I shall not need you again," she said.

"Very good, *mademoiselle*," said the footman with a stiff bow, and the car went away.

She was relieved about it, for not once in it had she felt

comfortable. And standing here she did not feel conspicuous at all, for people passed her by, now that the car was gone, with only that sidelong glance which is awarded every heart-stirring girl by the passerby.

Warm again and happy, she stepped off the walk and risked staining her tiny shoes in the grass. She felt she must walk in soft earth beneath a clear sky and feel clean wind, and so, for nearly an hour, she enjoyed herself.

Then she began to be aware of time slipping away from her. She knew she must compose herself, bring order to her activities, plan out each hour which remained to her. For only in that way could she stock a store of memories from which she could draw upon in the years which would remain to her.

Across the drive was a bench beside the lake and she knew that it would be a nice place to think and so she waited for the flow of traffic to abate so that she could cross to it.

She thought the way clear and stepped upon the street. There was a sudden scream of brakes and a thudding bump as wheels were stabbed into the gutter. She stood paralyzed with terror to see that a large car had narrowly missed her, and that only by expert driving on the part of its chauffeur.

A young man was out of the back and had her hand, dragging her from the street and into the car with him. She sat still, pale and weak, lips parted. But it was not from fright but from wonder. She had not wished for this and yet it could not have been better had she wished for it.

"You are not hurt?" he said. He was shy and nervous and when he saw that he still held her hand he quickly dropped it and moistened his lips.

She looked long at him. He was a young man, probably not more than twenty-five, for his skin was fresh and his eyes were clear. He radiated strength and this shyness of his was only born from fright at the near accident, fright for her and awe for her beauty as well. He was six feet tall and his eyes were black as his hair. His voice was low and showed breeding.

"Is there . . . there any place we can take you?"

"I . . . wasn't going anywhere in particular," she said. "You are very good. I . . . I am sorry I frightened you so. I wasn't watching—"

"It is all our fault," said the young man. "Please, may I introduce myself? I am Thomas Crandall."

"I am Meredith Smith."

"It . . . it isn't quite proper—to be introduced this way," he faltered. And then he smiled good-humoredly at her and they both began to laugh.

The laughter put them at ease and took away the memory of the near fatality.

They drove for a little while, more and more in tune with each other, and then he turned to her and asked, "Would I seem terribly bold if I asked you to have lunch with me? I at least owe you that."

"I would be very disappointed if you did not," she answered. "That . . . that isn't a very ladylike speech, I know, but . . . but I would like to have lunch with you."

He was flattered and enthralled and smiled it upon her. Most of his lingering shyness departed and he leaned toward the glass to tell his chauffeur, "The Montmaron, please."

"You know," he said a little while later as they sat in the

roof garden at a small table, "I was hoping that something like this might happen. Last night, I was hoping. Do you believe in wishes? I think wishes come true sometimes, don't they?"

She was startled that he might have read her secret, but she smiled at him and realized it wasn't so. The softness of the string music failed, after that, to wholly dispel a fear which had been implanted in her heart.

What would he think when he discovered— No, she mustn't dwell upon that. She would not dwell on the end.

He was so nice when he laughed. He was so nice.

And yet the knife of fear still probed her heart. He must not know. They would live up to the moment and then—then she—

"It's wine with bubbles in it," he was saying. "Wine with giggles in it. Drink a little but not too much."

She drank. She felt better. She almost forgot. . . .

They went to a matinee but she had so little attention for the stage that the play, afterward, seemed quite incoherent to her. Somehow Thomas Crandall was the leading man and Thomas Crandall occasionally smiled sideways at her. When it ended he was holding her hand. He seemed very doubtful of his small advances and she had the feeling that he was afraid he might touch her and break her.

"What will your family think?" he said when they were outside. "You've been gone all afternoon and someone must have expected you somewhere. Surely anyone as beautiful as you must be missed."

She felt nervous and guilty. "Oh . . . oh, I . . . I am not from New York. I am from Boston. That's it. From Boston.

And—my father and mother are both dead. I came down to see a show."

"Ah, so I've helped you attend to business." He grinned. "Then I am very much in luck. Then you can dine with me. And there are clubs and dancing and there will be a moon tonight—" Instantly he blushed. And she laughed at him.

"I am fond of the moon," she said, close against his arm. "Oh, but I must . . . must go to my hotel for a little while and dress."

"Tell Charles which one. No, tell me and I'll tell him. I should dress also."

"The . . . the Astor."

"I'll be back in an hour," he called to her from the curb. And the big car drew away.

She was filled with uneasiness to be standing there alone. She knew very little about such things and was certain she would make some mistake. But she reckoned without her beauty and the gallantry of man.

"I wish," she whispered to herself as she signed the register, "that I had a hundred dollars in my purse." And to the smiling clerk, "A suite, please. A large suite. My . . . my baggage will be brought in."

And the porter came through the door carrying new luggage with her name upon it.

When Thomas Crandall came back an hour later he stopped in wide-eyed reverence for the girl who came from the elevator. Her glowing chestnut hair swept down to naked shoulders and her gown, a graceful miracle in green, flowed closely

GET 4 FREE BOOKS!

You can have the titles in the Stories from the Golden Age delivered to your door by signing up for the book club. Start today, and we'll send you **4 FREE BOOKS** (worth $39.80) as your reward.

———◦◦———

The collection includes 80 volumes (book or audio) by master storyteller L. Ron Hubbard in the genres of science fiction, fantasy, mystery, adventure and western, originally penned for the pulp magazines of the 1930s and '40s.

———◦◦———

YES! ☑

Sign me up for the Stories from the Golden Age Book Club and send me my first book for $9.95 with my **4 FREE BOOKS** (FREE shipping). I will pay only $9.95 each month for the subsequent titles in the series. Shipping is FREE and I can cancel any time I want to.

_____ _____ _____
First Name   Middle Name   Last Name

_____
Address

_____ _____ _____
City   State   ZIP

_____ _____
Telephone   E-mail

Credit/Debit Card #: _____

Card ID# (last 3 or 4 digits): _____ Exp Date: _____/_____

Date (month/day/year) _____/_____/_____

Signature: _____

Comments: _____

Thank you!

To sign up online, go to: **www.GoldenAgeStories.com**

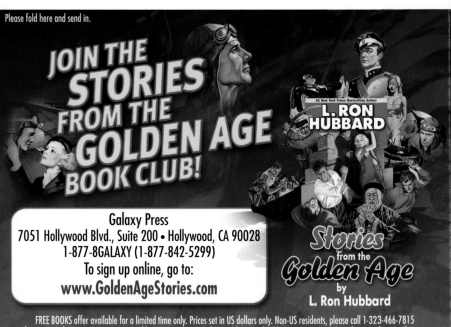

to her to sweep out and to the floor. Finding it difficult to speak—for there seemed to be something in his throat—he helped her into the ermine wrap and led her through the lobby and down the steps as though he were escorting the sun itself.

"You . . . you are beautiful," he said. "No, that's not adequate. You are— Oh," he gave it up, "where would you like to dine?"

"Where you are going?" she said.

He laughed. They both laughed. And they went away to dine.

The world became a fantasy of bright glasses and swirling color and music, a delicate sensory world, and people laughed together and waiters were quick and kind.

"Not too much," he admonished her. "It's not the wine. It's the bubbles. They have fantasies in them. Each one contains a giggle or a castle or the moon."

They danced. And the bubbles won.

Somewhat astonished she looked about her to find the last place nearly empty. A scrubwoman was already at work upon the floor and a man was piling tables and chairs. And the orchestra, when Tommy offered more largess, was too sleepy to play. There was no more champagne. There was no more music. And the edge of the roof garden was already gray and the moon had gone.

She yawned as he took her arm. She nearly fell asleep as they got into his car. She snuggled down against him and looked up at him.

He laughed at her and then grew serious. "If I thought . . . if . . . well . . . I wish I could marry you."

"Why can't you?" she said.

"Why can't— Do you mean it? But, no. You've known me a very short time. You—"

"I have known you forever. We are to be married!"

"But what if . . . if I turn out to be a drunkard?"

"Then I will also be a drunkard."

He looked at her for a moment. "You do love me, don't you, as I love you?"

She pulled his head down and kissed him.

Somewhat dazedly afterward he said to his chauffeur: "There must be a place where people can get married quickly."

"Quickly," she murmured.

"Yes, sir," said the chauffeur.

"Take us there," said Tommy.

Suddenly she was terrified. She did not dare permit him to do this. For in—in twenty-six hours she would be— But she was more afraid that he would not.

She snuggled against him once more and sighed. Twenty-six hours left. Only twenty-six hours left but they could be full and she could be happy. And somehow, she would have to have the courage to face what came after. To face the loss of him . . . she drowsed.

With sixteen hours left to her she lay upon the great bed in the airy room and looked at the ceiling beams where the afternoon sunlight sent reflections dancing. He had said that he had a few phone calls to make and that there would be a party beginning at six and that the whole city—or whoever was important in the city—would be there. And she had understood suddenly that she knew about Thomas Crandall or had heard of him as a playwright, fabulously successful.

This, his home, was a palace of wonder to her, all marble and teak and ivory, filled with servants who were soft-footed and efficient—servants of whom she was secretly in awe.

She had not wished this and yet it had happened. It had been all Tommy's idea to marry her, to bring her here, to give a great party. . . .

She did not have the courage it would take to run away now, before everyone came. For these hours were so precious that she hated to waste minutes in thinking so darkly on things. But think now she must. In sixteen hours she would be sixty-six years old, faded, delicate, starved— And Thomas Crandall—

She began to weep and, in a little while, realized that there was no solution. For what could she ask which she could retain? She could not plead that his love would not change. She knew that when he knew, he would be revolted both by her withered self and by the witchcraft which he would perceive. She could never stand to see him look at her as he would. And she could never bear to so cruelly abuse his love. For his love was not part of the wishes. If only it had been! Then he would forget—

And another knife of thought cut into her. Could she go back now, Mrs. Thomas Crandall, to a hovel on a sordid street and be happy with memory? She began to know that that could never be.

But his footstep was in the hall and he burst in followed by a train of servants who bore great boxes of clothes and flowers and little boxes full of things much more precious.

She was lost in the rapture of it. And then when she kissed him she forgot even the little boxes of velvet.

"Tommy, if this could last forever and ever—"

"It will last. Forever and ever." But he seemed to sense something strange in her and the dark eyes were thoughtful for just the space of a heartbeat. And her heart was racing.

"Tommy—don't leave me. Ever!"

"Never. In a little while the mayor and I don't know who all will be here for the wedding dinner. After your very slight wedding breakfast, I should think you would want something to eat. We'll have pheasants and . . . and hummingbird tongues—"

He scooped her up and carried her around the room and pretended to throw her out of the window.

And so the hours fled, as vanishes a song.

And it was four o'clock in the morning with the summer day heralded by a false dawn. Beside her Tommy slept quietly, hair tousled, one arm flung across her. A bird began to chirp himself into groggy wakefulness and somewhere in the direction of the river a boat whistled throatily. A clock was running in the room. Running loudly. She could just see its glowing face and knew that it was four. She had just four hours left. Four hours.

And she could not trust herself. She had to run away. But she could not trust herself not to afterward come back. And everything she had been given would be taken away except the memory.

The memory!

She knew now that a memory was not enough. A memory would be pain she could not bear. She would read of his plays. And hear of his continued fame. And she—she would not be able to come near him—and she would not be able to stay away. She would come back and he would not believe her. He would turn her forth and she would see a look upon his face—

She shivered.

She knew suddenly what she had to do and so she shivered.

With gentle slowness, she removed his arm and crept from the bed. He stirred and seemed about to wake and then quieted. She bent and kissed his cheek and a small bright tear glowed there in the cold false dawn. He stirred again and muttered her name in his sleep. A frown passed over his brow and then again he was still.

She drew her robe about her and tiptoed out into the anteroom where she quickly dressed. She commanded pen and ink:

My Darling:

This has all been a dream and I am grateful. You must not think of me again for I am not worth the thought. I knew I could not be with you past this dawn and yet I allowed your love for me to grow. Darling, try to forgive me. I go into nothingness. Do not think of me as unfaithful for I shall be faithful. But I was given forty-eight hours of freedom and now— By the time you read this I shall be dead. Do not search for me. It cannot be otherwise. I am grateful to you. I love you.

Meredith

At six, Tommy Crandall woke with a terrified start. He did not know what had happened but he seemed to hear a far-off voice cry to him. Meredith was gone. He flung back the covers and leaped up to search madly for her. A valet looked strangely at him.

"Mrs. Crandall left here two hours ago, sir. She went in a taxi. She said she had left you a note— Here it is, sir."

Tommy read the note and then, trembling, read it through again. He walked in a small circle in the middle of the room and then suddenly understood. Wildly he snatched at his clothes and got them on.

"Get the car!" he roared at the valet. "Oh, my God, get the car! I'll find her. I have to find her!"

He did not bother to go to the Astor, for there was an urgency in the note which directed his steps immediately to the police.

And he found a sleepy sergeant at the morgue who yawned as he said, "You can look but we ain't got nothing like that in here. Two firemen that burned up on a ship and a couple of accident cases come in about dawn. But we ain't got no beautiful woman. No, sir, it ain't very often you see a beautiful woman down here. When they're beautiful they don't let themselves—"

Tommy flung away and then turned. "How do I find a medical examiner?"

"That's a thought," yawned the sergeant. "Call headquarters and they'll give you the duty desk."

It was eight o'clock before Tommy found the medical examiner who knew. The man was still perturbed and perplexed, for he was not at ease about things. He was a small, nervous politician's heel dog.

He ran a finger under his collar as he gazed at the overwrought young man who stood in the doorway. "Well, I thought it was irregular. But it was my duty and there was no sign of foul play. And so I took the death certificate and signed it—"

Tommy turned pale. "Then . . . then she is dead."

"Why, yes. A funny thing," said the coroner uncomfortably. "But she came and got me and said to come along and, of course, a beautiful woman that way and looking rich, I went along. And we came to this undertaking parlor and went in and she said she had two hundred and twenty dollars of her own money. She was very particular about its being her own money and she—"

"Are you sure she is dead?"

"Why, yes, I say, she made the arrangements on the condition that she would be buried right away without a notice sent out or anything and paid spot cash and then—well, she dropped dead."

"How do you know?"

"Brother, when they're dead, they're dead. My stethoscope doesn't lie. And no sign of foul play or poison whatever. And, well, I took my pen in hand and signed. She didn't want an autopsy because she said she couldn't stand being cut up, and she didn't want to be embalmed. So they just took her and buried—"

"What funeral parlor?" demanded Tommy savagely.

"I'll give you the address," said the examiner. And he did.

The professional manner of the undertaker Tommy dashed aside. "A lady by the name of Meredith Smith Crandall was here this morning."

"Why, yes," said the sad gentleman. "Yes, that is true." He looked upset. "Is there anything wrong?"

"No. Nothing wrong—no trouble for you, I mean. What happened?"

"Why, she came in and paid for a funeral on the condition that she would be buried right away and so we buried her, of course. She paid cash, double price on our cheapest funeral. She insisted it was her own money. I don't know why. The thing is very regular. We have a certificate—"

"Take me to the cemetery!" cried Tommy in anguish.

"Certainly," said the undertaker respectfully. "But she has been legally buried and an exhumation order—"

"Take me there!"

They drove between the gateposts of Woodpine and it was twenty minutes of ten. The undertaker pointed to the grave where the turf was still raw. A workman was starting to clear away to put sod on the place and another was hauling away spare dirt.

The undertaker looked at Tommy with amazement. The workmen stared. Tommy immediately seized a spade and began to throw back the earth. When they attempted to stop him he struck at them with the implement and kept on digging. And then, because his very savageness had cowed them, they helped him lift the cheap, sealed coffin from the earth. Tommy knocked off the lid with the spade.

A little old lady lay there, clad in decent if ragged garments, her fine gray hair a halo above the delicate oval of her face. But she was not lying with crossed arms. And she had not died with a smile. She had been so tiny that she had been able to turn over in her coffin and now she lay, with a bruised and bloodied face and torn hands, huddled on her side, and her expression did not indicate that she had died in peace.

It was ten o'clock.

The workmen suddenly drew away from Tommy. The undertaker gasped and involuntarily crossed himself. For the man who clutched the body to him and wept was no longer young. He was an old man of more than sixty now where he had been young before, and the good garments he had worn had become carefully kept but threadbare tweed. What hair he had now was gray. And the tears which coursed down his cheeks made their way through furrows put there by loneliness and privation.

You see, Georgie had made two calls the day before.

The Devil's Rescue

The Devil's Rescue

HE had been cold so long that he had even ceased to dream of the great logs crackling in the old manor fireplace of his home. He just shivered now and then and ached, becoming conscious of the fact that it was bitter for a moment and then relapsing into a blue ache which ate him from the mop of his salt-encrusted hair to his cracked feet.

He had stopped courting the madness of envisioning great dinners he had eaten, recalling rather the peculiarly delicious flavor of the last biscuit in the breadbox, which moldy and inedible had vanished to its last crumb some two days before.

At the end of sixty hours he had been exhausted with holding himself against the sick lurches, the violent pitches and whipping rolls of the nineteen-foot lifeboat but now he braced himself not at all but lay prone in five inches of water and limply shifted with it from side to side.

It was hell to open his eyes once the salt had formed over them while shut, but some deep instinct in him bade him, now and then, to look up at the tattered ensign which hung upside down on the mast. The savage energy of the wind tearing into the red and white and blue wool wearied him and again he shut his eyes.

It was almost sunset. Sunset of his twenty-second day in

an open boat somewhere south and west of that ironically named place, the Cape of Good Hope.

First he had unloaded the cabin boy over the rail and into the grey restlessness of the sea. He had done it with great sorrow at the time, although it seemed to him now that the important thing about it was how strong he had been. What determination had shone out of him that he would not suffer a like fate! How bravely had he braced himself against that oar, bidding the crew bend their backs until the wind shifted and he could set the sail.

Then he had unloaded the cook. It had seemed strange that the fellow had not been able to live longer on his fat. And the wind hadn't shifted and when dawn rose, the reason why he'd had to carry so much starboard helm the last hour became apparent and so they had dumped the bow oar into the sea.

That was all after the wind had started to blow straight off the Cape. There was nothing astern but auks, he told them. Auks and ice, and they had nothing to lose but their lives which weren't worth much anyway. And so they'd dumped the bow oar's dead heaviness into the sea, whipped into a creamy froth now by the rising wind.

About then he had ceased keeping track of the rest of his crew. The captain, had he not been dead on the schooner's house and in a hundred fathom by now, would have kept a very punctual log about it, doubtless. But not his mate.

And then a couple or five days ago he had finally gotten tired of watching an arm swing back and forth from the thwart, and to still an urge which demanded to discover if man was fair food, hitched himself upright and, after an hour's work, had managed to slide the body into the thick of a craggy wave which gulped and gave up its prey no more.

He had stared in stupefaction, then, at the biscuit which floated upon the sea water in the bilge. He wondered that the bosun had not eaten it long before. But the bosun's loss was his gain and so he had eaten.

The foolishness of eating came to him afterwards. For eating would prolong his life yet a little while and he was heartily sick of the way the boat kept lurching, rolling, pitching. If the sail hadn't blown away long ago he would have tried to steady the thing with it.

The sound of the wind had gotten into his head along with the slap of the single remaining halyard and he was certain that he would never be able to get it out again. The sea, too, made far too much tumult, for each time a wave towered up its forty feet the wind hacked it down again and sent the top hissing straight out until the air was a horizontal sheet of water, discoloring the already leaden sky.

Wondering a little at his energy now, he put in a time at bailing, scooping up some water, lifting the can to the gunwale, spilling it out, bringing it back, scooping it up, lifting it to the gunwale, spilling it out, bringing it back, scooping it up, spilling it out, lifting it to the gunwale. . . .

He stared for a little at his empty hand, thinking dully that the sea must be still hungry after swallowing eight corpses one after the other. A small part of him was alarmed for now the boat would fill, little by little, at last to sink. The greater part of him said with some relief that, well, he wouldn't have to bail anymore anyway.

Why he didn't get pneumonia or die of cold like the others was a problem which he would not now have to solve. That would save his head a lot of useless work. For a man had no right to live at all somewhere off Good Hope in the awfulness of its winter with the ferocity of its gales and the chill of its water; not even a bucko mate in the full strength of his twenty-five years.

The streak of irony in his nature had risen up many times to aid him and perhaps in it there was some small explanation of why he had outlasted those sturdy but stolid souls to whom death was simply death and not a rather good joke on the unwary.

After all, he pondered in one of his few wholly lucid moments, what more could he ask? For a good five hours he had had a command, for when the mast had been shivered, striking down the captain, it had been his lot to valiantly strive to keep the schooner afloat with pumps which took out only half of what came in through the sprung seams.

And now again he had a command, his solitary own, nineteen feet in length, seven feet in beam. And what mattered it if he was riding to the slashed sails and boom which made up the sea anchor? What mattered it if there were now eight good inches of water to slosh in the bottom, over the bottom boards continually and over himself at least half of the time?

The clearness of thought began to seep from him and he stared half unseeing at wind-split Old Glory.

The whole thing was impossible and he achieved the belief that he, Edward Lanson, was not here at all, that neither Cape of Good Hope nor South Atlantic existed. Somebody had made a very great mistake and had hung up the wrong scenery around him. He wasn't he and the sea existed not at all. The dark which dropped so slowly, coming down like the easy fingers of death, would take everything away and he would awake in a dry bed to a breakfast fit for a sailor, finding that this had been nothing but nightmare.

He had dreamed the clammy flesh of the dead as he jettisoned them. He had dreamed the weeping of the cabin boy who wept only because of the sorrow his mother would feel. He had dreamed even the *Gloucester Maid*.

He came to himself at the wrench of a powerful sea. It was quite dark now but over him the wind screamed and about him crashed the sea, unbelievable in its power to destroy, conscienceless in its voracity.

He roused himself, for now the bilge covered his face at each roll and though he could not discover any reason for not strangling and thereby putting a swift period to his pain, it took less energy to lift himself with his back to the 'midship thwart than it did to force himself to lie and die.

There was ice in the spray which rattled against his back and he fished listlessly around until he retrieved somebody's sou'wester. The feel of it was clammy but after a while he got used to it.

His chin sunk hopelessly upon his breast; he rode out the thundering hours, coming to himself now and then and remaining for whole minutes with his wits more clear than they had ever before been in all his life. He thought of the time he had wasted, the countless easy hours spent wholly without purpose, and somehow it amused him to know that all men squander their time, purblind to the hour, often close at hand, when precious few minutes and seconds would be theirs to spend.

The water was now up to his waist as he sat, a full fourteen inches above the bottom boards, eighteen from the keel. Its shifting weight made the craft stagger and take on even more until sometimes half the gunwale was alight with a phosphorescent gleam of foaming spray. The movement pulled him back and forth so that he had to brace himself a little with his arms along the thwart; he had not the strength to adjust himself completely.

If he had ever been close to the shipping lanes, he was far from them now, beyond any possibility of rescue. As he was driven southward he approached Antarctica and the days, each after the last, would increase their cold and the wind its content of ice. A thousand or four thousand miles away was Hobart. A thousand or five hundred directly into the whip of the gale which drove him off was Cape Town. Somehow it was strange to know that actual solid land was still in existence upon the planet, that ships still plowed the deep, that he still lived when all these others were long dead.

It must have been close to eleven in that wailing night when he saw a light. Raised high on the crest and then dropped into the trough as he was continually, it was a sketchy glimpse. Stubbornly he would not allow himself to know it for he full realized that the disappointment would be too agonizing for his remaining sanity to bear.

And yet, each time he was hurtled dizzily in the dark to the foam-toothed peaks, he glimpsed the light anew. Before long, though still refusing to wholeheartedly support the sight, he began to ponder its source, for certainly it resembled no beacon, nor did it seem to be either a running or a range light, for its color was not red or green or white but rather a pale yellow admixed with green. And it was not of one source but rather of many.

At last he believed fully in it and reserved his judgment only about rescue, for it was not to be borne that a ship should pass so near without sighting him.

Now, in these minutes when, believe it whether he would, he might possibly be hauled dripping from the maw of death, his mind refused to function, embattled in itself between desire and refusal to hope.

Ship or land, whichever, it bore steadily toward him, growing better defined with each soaring heave of the sea around. It grew larger but no brighter.

He had known of men going mad in an open boat and seeing all manner of things and then turning berserk when they refused to be real; and it seemed to him that some satanic plan was afloat to draw him into a few croaking cheers after which the vision would vanish. But perhaps if he still refused and did not cheer at all, then he himself would be the victor, outwitting the hostile jokester who saw fit to so work this thing upon him.

He had averted cannibalism. Now, praise God, could he stave off madness, too? He would be cunning. He would rest his chin upon his breast and give no sign and when at last it was too near to withdraw he would seize upon it and so win his life.

Thus, covertly, did he come to believe in the thing and his mind, freed from the struggle, kindled with knowledge that dry in the locker in the stern sheets were four flares. Without betraying any anxiety, he made his way over the thwarts and lifted the cover. His hands were still and raw and it took him some time to finally pull the cap from one with sufficient force to ignite the cap.

Hotly it smoldered, blinding him when it broke into light. He was startled by the sight of the tumbling seas and the frailty of the half-sunken lifeboat. The enormity of his plight rose up into his throat.

He shielded his eyes from the glare and again sought the thing. He could not see it so plainly now but he knew that it was closer. Strange the outline it had taken on, for the whole affair was aglow and it appeared to be nothing more than a triangle of pale fire.

Certainly no ship, however staunch, could plow directly into the gale, squaresa'ls set even to t'gal'nts!

And certainly those bluff bows and reaching sprit belonged to no staid grain ship, relic of far-gone days when sail was mistress!

The warmth of the flare was good to his hand. He noted its feeling carefully for still he had no faith in this thing. Reason stated that it could not exist and, if it did, that it could not sail in such a fashion and, if it did, would never be booming up from Antarctica.

But there it was, growing larger, and he fancied that, above the yell of wind, he could make out a repeated hail and the creak of straining gear. Then, in an abrupt lull, he heard the thunder of slacked canvas, amid which a voice clearly cried, "Ahoy the whaleboat! Stand by to take a line!"

It was a trick of the sea, that order. It was a failure in his head that the old merchantman was standing to on his windward to drift down upon him with the wind and sea. But all too plainly he heard the canvas booming now as it was momentarily spilled of wind.

The flare did not seem to affect the strange glow which outlined the entire craft, but as the vessel neared he saw that the sails were scarlet, not yellow green, and that the masts were black, gleaming with spray.

A line whistled by his ear and a monkey fist plunked into a wave beyond him. He was almost afraid, in a sudden fit of premonition which stood up the hair along his neck, to touch that heaving line. The moment's lull was chased away by the returning scream of wind and once the hemp was in his hand he was frightened at the thought of letting it go.

Swiftly he hauled it to him, unmindful of the pain of it through his raw palms. The hawser thumped on the gunwale and he brought it up to carry it forward and drop it over a bitt.

"Haul away!" he cried, his own voice sounding thick but small. The jerk on the lifeboat slammed him to the thwart and he hung on, staring up at the nearing vessel, split apart as he was by the desire to continue his life and the knowledge that this was somehow an awful thing.

At the rail were many faces, unearthly white against the glowing scarlet of the canvas. Not a sound came from them now. He could feel the intensity of eyes upon him and the atmosphere of the vessel reached out and clothed him in clammy garments.

A line dropped down beside him and he placed the bowline on the bight about both his seat and his shoulders and presently, as the sea dropped away with his boat, he felt himself hauled swiftly up.

Hands pulled him down from the rail to the deck and, ordinarily, at this moment of salvation, he would have given way to an intense desire to lean upon their support. But of their faces he could make out nothing save blots of glowing white.

Not a word was spoken until one sailor, drawing his knife, made as if to cut away the lifeboat.

"Don't!" cried Lanson in sudden horror.

All faces turned to him.

"Haul it astern," he begged. "It's not much to tow and . . . and it's my only command."

The knife poised over the hawser for seconds and then the sailor withdrew it and thrust it again into his belt.

Lanson looked up and down the deck, anxious to confront an officer and be told that what he thought was untrue and that this greeting was only a trick of his exhausted nerves.

By the mast he saw a larger fellow, seated and seemingly

disinterested, passing a marlinespike from fist to fist. A visored cap sat upon his head and Lanson stumbled toward him, hoping that here was the mate, a man with a face.

But the mate had no face whatever.

"I am Edward Lanson, mate of the schooner *Gloucester Maid,* foundered three weeks or more ago off Cape of Good Hope."

The fellow turned up his featureless face and continued to pass the marlinespike back and forth. Finally he made a motion with his head toward the quarterdeck and Lanson found himself supported in that direction by the members of the crew.

Any exultation he had felt in his rescue was spent now for it was all too apparent that this ship, hemp-rigged, low of waist and high of stern and fo'c's'le, should have ceased to sail centuries before.

The crew stopped at the bottom of the ladder to the poop and Lanson looked up to find a tall, nervous fellow up there, dressed in an ancient Spanish mode with the silver hilts of pistols protruding from his sash and rapier sweeping back in a thin, bright line. But here, thank God, was a face!

"The *Gloucester Maid,* Edward Lanson, mate, sir."

"Dead?"

"My crew, sir, my crew and my captain every one."

The man on the upper deck took a restless pace back and forth before he faced Lanson again. The dark eyes flamed strangely.

"This is ill done, Mister Mate. Dead, you say, every one but you?"

"Aye."

"Foundered off the Cape?"

"Aye."

"And adrift three weeks in an open boat."

"Aye."

"You . . . you have no curiosity about the deck on which you stand?"

"I would rather not, sir. I am weary."

"Of course! But you are a prudent man, Mister Mate. And you would lie if you said you did not know that before you stands Captain Vanderbeck."

Lanson's knees were buckling with exhaustion and only the hands held him erect.

"Take him below," said Vanderbeck. "Give him stout wine. Madeira with a little pilot bread broken in it. When he wakes give him food." He did not have to raise his voice to get above the wind.

He turned about and paced into the dark of the quarterdeck while the sailors eased Lanson down a companionway and so into a bunk. Presently one came and gave him the medicine prescribed and then, when the door was shut and he was alone, Lanson let his head sink into the pillow and out of him seeped all concern, fleeing before the delicious desire to sleep forever.

When he awoke he found that he still could feel the uneven lurching of the lifeboat, so long had he endured it. The motion was at variance with that of this ancient merchantman and he made very unsteady progress out of the bunk. It was with surprise that he found it dark outside his port and he wondered if he could have slept through twenty-four hours. In any case he was very refreshed compared to what he had been and he drank some more wine and ate a little pilot bread and began to wonder if any more solid fare would be offered.

His clothes had been rinsed, he found, in fresh water and now hung upon a rack, almost dry. He washed his sore body in a bucket placed there for that purpose and used a half of the bottle of salve which had been left beside the bucket; it cooled his salt-stung skin and allowed him to move without wincing. All the while the cabin kept going up and down and back and forth, duplicating the ceaseless motion of the lifeboat, though when he steadied himself against these expected lunges, he only upset his own balance which was overcome by the steadier movement of the vessel itself.

In a little while, when he was at last dressed and ready, as though somebody had been watching him all the while, the faceless mate put his head in at the door. He said no word but extended a scrap of parchment on which was written:

> You will do me the favor of dining in my cabin.
>   Vanderbeck

"What day is this?" said Lanson.

But the mate withdrew without a word and his sea boots left no sound in the passageway. Lanson turned to a mirror and nervously fixed the knot in his sailor's scarf.

All his life he had had an uncanny awareness of time so that no matter the circumstances he was always able to count off the bells without the aid of a watch. As he came more clearly himself he realized that there was something very wrong in its being night and though he had no true check of it he felt that his sleep had been of at least thirty-six hours duration. Remembering, he knew that he had awakened three or four times, each time to find a watcher at his side, ready with a warm broth. But it was all indistinct as though it had happened to another.

He combed his long hair with his fingers and then fell to studying his face, not really wanting to for fear of what he might discover. But there was life in his dark eyes, color in his sunken cheeks and lips. No, there was no doubt about his being still alive, no more than there was any doubt about his recovery.

He fingered the note and pondered the captain's name, summing up what he had already seen and heard. And then, suddenly he sank down on the edge of his bed and cupped his face in his worn hands.

What release did he have now?

Why hadn't they let him die out there alone?

For it was quite clear to Edward Lanson now that he faced an endless life of storm in the company of a madman with a crew long dead!

The door swung silently inward and the impassive mate was there again, gesturing mildly that Lanson was to follow without more delay. Lanson avoided looking at the white expanse between cap and collar, at the fingers with their all-too-prominent joints. He followed.

The main cabin was ornate with carved blackwood furniture, glowing silks and oriental carpets. Along the bulkheads to either side were rows of chests, camphor and ivory and teak, from which drooled the luster of pearls or gaped a little over a load of dull gold coins. The ports were twenty feet athwartship and full seven feet tall, all of cunningly set glass to make compasses and tritons and sea horses; through this, trailing far behind them, glowed their frothing wake, leading off into the gray dark and the shrieking wind.

Before Lanson paid heed to the occupants of the room he searched for and found the lifeboat, planing behind them from its taut painter.

Vanderbeck stood with his back to the companionway, staring gloomily through the stern ports. When Lanson touched the back of a chair, making a slight noise, the captain turned slowly. He had taken off pistols and rapier and had changed sea boots for buckled slippers but he was still garbed in black silk which gave his face an unnatural glow.

"Wine?" said Vanderbeck.

"As you will," said Lanson.

The captain waved him into a seat at the table but did not himself sit down. Watching the man's restive pacing, Lanson broke some dried fruit in his hands and chased it down with excellent port.

"You are a fellow of remarkable indestructibility," said Vanderbeck.

"I might," ventured Lanson, "say the same of you."

"Yes . . . yes, that's so, I suppose. But blast me, Mister Mate, if I'd enjoy twenty-one days in an open boat, dumping over the crew one by one."

"I . . . I'd rather not talk about it, sir, if you please."

"Yes, yes, yes, of course! Blast me, of course! Good fruit, eh?"

"Very tasty."

"Good, good. Got it from a derelict named the *Martha Howe*. Captain must have been a fool to desert her. There she was, floating high and where was he? Shark bait, most likely. A joke on the fellow, eh?"

Lanson drank a little more wine.

"Marvelous what one finds bobbing around," said Vanderbeck. "God love us, a man begins to believe that the accursed world is only intent upon one thing—giving all their riches to Old Man Sea."

"I suppose one would think so," said Lanson, "looking at all these chests."

"These? Rubble, Mister Mate. I should show you what there is in the forward hold. But here's the dinner." He sat down and the sailor who had entered laid the board with smoothly mechanical motions. His face too was featureless.

"But what worth is it?" demanded Vanderbeck. "It can't be spent. It can't buy me what *I* want! Have some beef."

Lanson ate as slowly as he could, experiencing difficulty with an insane desire to snatch out with both hands and bolt everything in sight. Neither of them said anything more until they had finished and the steward had brought forth some liquors and coffee.

Vanderbeck sank back in his chair and examined his watch, comparing it with an ancient chronometer on another table a short distance away. While he was so engaged a shadow was thrown in the path of the swinging lamp. Lanson's liquor glass slopped a little.

The captain of the *Gloucester Maid,* recognizable only by his clothes, having no slightest feature from chin to brow, stood deferentially at Vanderbeck's chair. Lanson felt that he was being looked upon but he tried to make no sign.

"Course eas'-nor'-eas' and wind strong, sir," said the captain of the *Gloucester Maid.*

"Eas'-nor'-eas'," repeated Vanderbeck. "When do we pass the Cape?"

"At midnight, sir."

"Perhaps," said Vanderbeck, "we'll not be turned back this time. Steady as you go."

The *Gloucester Maid*'s master touched his cap and withdrew.

"And maybe we will," said Vanderbeck. "That's the only hope. To pass the Cape and be quit of this forever. Hah, Mister Mate, we'll have a drink on it for I very much fear that your own fate also depends upon it."

Lanson drank with him.

"Perhaps," said Vanderbeck, growing more expansive, "*he'll* not even board us this night!"

Lanson smiled. "Has *he* ever failed?"

Vanderbeck clouded, glancing around. "Must you rob me of even the wish? No, *he's* never failed. Not in all these hundreds of years. But by this watch *he's* close to ten minutes overdue. That's unusual."

They lapsed into silence, both of them waiting, Lanson knowing full well who was coming and why and marveling slightly that he in his youth should be wise in lore so old.

He did not disappoint them, though the time had progressed almost an hour. There was a swirl of wind upon the deck, even louder than the already shrieking gale. The ship was, for a moment, in the grip of some savage force which strained at it and made it reel.

There came a sound of great boots on the deck and a halloo for Vanderbeck. Vanderbeck sat still.

The boots made the companionway groan and the room was full of rushing wind and glaring light and smoke too. Lanson looked steadily at his glass.

"What's this?" said an ingratiating voice.

"Edward Lanson," said Vanderbeck.

"And who, may I politely ask, is Edward Lanson?"

"Hah!" said Vanderbeck. "Is he as good as that?" He laughed immoderately, and then, "Mate of the *Gloucester Maid,* or perhaps I should say captain since he had the command for five hours. A cool one, my friend, and worthy of *your* notice. He outlives all the men in his boat. . . ."

"By taking their rations for himself?" hopefully.

Lanson's face was very stiff when he looked up. The *fellow* in the dark, dripping cloak had slunk into a chair and *his* pointed brows were raised half amusedly, half cynically.

"*You* do not know everything, I see," said Lanson coldly.

"*You* see?" cried Vanderbeck. "*You* see? Twenty-one days in an open boat and he comes up with enough nerve to bait *you!*" Laughter shook him so that, pouring wine, the bottle chattered against the glass.

He was not cross. A leer of disbelief appeared upon his tapering face. "No man, my young mate, has any such remarkable power of self-sacrifice. *I* should know for, after all, *I* govern the lives of more than you suppose."

"But not mine," said Lanson, "and so I'll not be made to take that lie. Though I can't say that *your* good opinion is of any great importance to me."

Vanderbeck poured brandy all around in his enthusiasm. *He* looked put out and not at all pleased with what Vanderbeck had done.

"This was poorly thought of," *he* growled.

"What can I do? *You* rob me, one by one, of those I get to man her. Even tonight the time of five is through and so they leave with *you*. And when I go to the work of lying to, shall I desist because, wonder of wonders, he is not dead?"

"What else can he expect now?"

"*You'll* give him the same chance as others," said Vanderbeck. "He boards me and he is not afraid. Nor is he even afraid of *you*! And therefore *you* wish him ill. He'll have the same chance, I say."

He peered at Lanson with shifty eyes but Lanson only sipped his brandy and did not blink. He despised the *fellow* from the nethermost reaches of his soul.

After a little, *he* got up and wandered about the room, opening the chests and regaining *his* good spirits by laughing at the contents. The sight of gold and gems reacted upon *him* like a colossal prank. Finally *he* took heed of the chronometer and sat down at the table again.

From inside the cloak *he* took a great dice cup and wrapping *his* long fingers over the edge, made the cubes within dance.

"Always *your* dice," said Vanderbeck. "As the years go by I trust *you* less and less."

"Pah, you think *my* dice are false? Here! Inspect them!"

83

"What good would that do?" said Vanderbeck. "But, this time, won't *you* use mine?"

"And be certain, then, that they are false? What a child you think *me*, Captain Vanderbeck. High man for first?"

"As *you* will," said Vanderbeck.

Promptly *he* rolled out four sixes and a five and sat there grinning while Vanderbeck took the great box and made the cubes rattle. When they fell upon the cloth they showed but small numbers.

"Shoot first, then," cried Vanderbeck, "and be damned to *you*. This night I'll pass the Cape, that I swear!"

"Have you not sworn too much already, perhaps?" *he* said. Vanderbeck flushed.

He rolled the dice and got three fives. The remaining two presently bounced forth and one of them was a five. The last was also a mate to the rest.

"Five fives," *he* grinned. "Shoot five sixes now and pass the Cape. Yes, shoot five sixes or five aces and be free of it. Rattle them well, Captain Vanderbeck, for again you near land after long cruising. Fail and you are *mine* for seven years more."

Vanderbeck's eyes were overbright. "*You've* never been beaten. *You* have no concern. And it only amuses *you* to see another try. But here, I'll shoot and to hell with *you*."

The five dice leaped from the box and when they had quieted they read two sixes, a pair of fours and a deuce. Vanderbeck's hands shook when he laid the sixes aside and put the trio back into the cup. Thoroughly he shook them, savagely he threw them. Two more sixes came to view.

He was still grinning, self-assured. It amused *him* to see the moistness of Vanderbeck's hands and the tremble of the captain's lip.

Vanderbeck sent the die spinning round and round inside the cup and then, as though abandoning everything, let it fall to sight.

He began to laugh in a quiet, horrible sort of way. Vanderbeck's eyes were starting from their sockets and he appeared to be on the verge of insanity. Lanson whirled the brandy in the glass with small motions.

"Four sixes and a deuce won't do it *I'm* afraid," *he* said. "And so you're *mine* another seven years. But worry not. Again *I'll* bless your ship. She shall not founder. No, she'll carry you through the storm of winds which blow around the bottom of the world and we'll not meet again until your time has once more come. And so, good voyage to you, Captain Vanderbeck. Collect your crews upon the sea and send them on when their time is done. After all, you gave ship and self to *me* to win against these seas. You won, you see. And so, goodbye and good sailing. . . ."

"There's the matter of myself," said Lanson quietly. He dared not hope. "After all, I had no part in this and offered nothing to the sea but my own small strength. I come here only by chance and *you* have no right to keep me."

"Blast me, that's true," said Vanderbeck. "Much as I like you, Mister Mate, I like you a shade too well to have you so condemned. Come, *you*, he'll have to have his chance."

He regarded them uncertainly for a little and then smiled in an oily fashion, slipping sideways into the chair once more.

"You really want to be given back to the sea, Edward Lanson?"

"Rather that than this."

"Then you do not like *my* service."

"I did not ask to enter it."

His eyes shifted from the direct stare and *he* again produced the dice cup. "But let it be understood what you do. You shoot for your freedom and *I* for your soul. Is that correct?"

Lanson sat up a little straighter and took a hitch on his nerve. "Yes."

"High man shoots first."

And *he* rolled four sixes and a trey.

Lanson took the box. He stared for a while into its depths and then stirred it up. He tossed and got a hotchpotch of small ones.

He took the box again, rotating it slowly, all the while grinning triumphantly at Lanson. When the dice spewed forth there were three aces, a four and a deuce. *His* quick hands tossed the four and the deuce back and when they leaped out again they were an ace and a trey. *He* placed the fourth ace with the first three and the die went round and round inside the cup while *he* enjoyed Lanson's strained face. Then it bounced to the board and teetered for a moment between an ace and a six. Then it fell, the ace on the side.

He shrugged. "Four aces to beat, Edward Lanson. But even if you lose *I* am not such a hard master."

"I have not lost," said Lanson stubbornly.

He made the dice clatter in the cup. With a twitch of his wrist he scattered them on the green cloth. Two aces were there to be set aside. *He* tittered. "Go ahead, Edward Lanson. As you say, you have not lost."

Lanson rattled the three dice savagely. He spilled them and when they had stopped, only one was found to be an ace.

"Keep right on," *he* laughed. "Not even yet have you lost."

Lanson shot *him* a contemptuous glare. The two remaining dice leaped about in the box and then bounced swiftly forth.

Vanderbeck leaped up so suddenly that he upset his brandy, "*You* see!" he cried. "*You* see! Two aces and that makes five! He's shot five aces and he's got *you*! Then *you can* be beaten. *You* can! And seven years from tonight when we again come near the Cape, we'll see!"

But a strange thing was happening to Lanson. *His* evil face was beginning to fade. Vanderbeck was beginning to fade. The very tapestries of the room were growing indistinct.

The steward who waited in the door became only a boney thing and then a shadow and finally vanished altogether. The beams overhead grew as transparent as glass and even Vanderbeck's voice was drawing far off.

The *face* was gone. The chests were gone. The table and the beef were gone. And then the deck under his feet was nothing and he began to fall.

The water was a bitter shock. A hungry wave towered up and dropped its tons of froth upon him. He came to the surface gasping and struck out wildly, encumbered by his clothes, smothered by the sea, deafened by the wind.

Close beside him something white was bobbing and he clung desperately to it. The solidity of the canvas-wrapped spar was reassuring for he knew it as a sea anchor. More calmly now he worked himself up the line to the lifeboat's bow, discovering that he was only using one hand.

It took some time for him to get over the lunging gunwale but at last he lay in the half-swamped boat, gasping with relief.

Presently he pulled himself to the 'midship thwart and lay out flat upon it. There was something to which he had clung and now he gazed wonderingly upon it, finding that he still held a dice box.

Overhead the winds that howl around the bottom of the world tore spray straight out from the crests of every wave until a solid sheet of water was continually in the air. Back and forth, up and down, rolling, pitching and staggering, the lifeboat floundered through the gale.

Lanson got in the sea anchor and hung its beribboned canvas upon the mast as best he could, the while glancing about for any further sign of the spectral *Flying Dutchman*.

But the sea was clear, and after a little he lashed the helm upon a northerly course. Gripping the dice box with a stubborn hand and kneeling on the buried bottom boards, Edward Lanson began to bail.

Story Preview

NOW that you've just ventured through some of the captivating tales in the Stories from the Golden Age collection by L. Ron Hubbard, turn the page and enjoy a preview of *The Tramp*. Join Doughface Jack, who acquires phenomenal mental powers after a brain operation—now he can instantaneously heal, kill or make the old young. Goaded by a vengeful and beautiful woman, Doughface is propelled headlong towards the ultimate seat of power!

The Tramp

"FOR a man that's been through what happened to you, I'd say you looked marvelous," smiled Miss Finch. That was not exactly true. Doughface had always been as fat as a butterball and his complexion had never been anything but pasty white. The bluish growth of beard did not help.

"What's the idea?" said Doughface, glancing around again.

"You mean where are you?" said Miss Finch. "Doctor Pellman saw you get hurt and brought you here. He operated."

"Geez," said Doughface, alarmed, "I ain't got no lucre. Them things cost the bucks!"

"Never mind," said Miss Finch. "The doctor hasn't collected a bill for years and he doesn't even try anymore. You can thank him for your life."

"Huh," said Doughface, "he must be a right guy."

"He's a wonderful fellow, if that's what you mean," said Miss Finch.

"Y'mean I'd be dead if it wasn't fer him, huh?"

"That's it."

"Geez . . . And he don't want no lucre for it?"

"No," replied Miss Finch. "Now you be quiet and I'll go get you something to eat."

"Eat?"

"Yes. Anything you want in particular?"

91

Doughface shut his eyes and then gathered courage to take the plunge. "How about chicken and ice cream?"

"All right," said Miss Finch.

Doughface blinked. He suspected this wasn't Earth after all. If it wasn't for that mole this girl would look just like . . . Huh! He gaped at her in astonishment.

"What's the matter?" said Miss Finch.

"That . . . uh . . . y'had a mole on yer chin and it ain't there no more!"

Her hand flew to the spot. She stepped to a mirror at the head of the bed and stared at herself. "Why . . . why, that's so. It's gone!"

Through it all the man on one side had not moved and neither had the girl practically hidden in bandages.

Doughface did not long concentrate on the vanishing mole. "What burg is this?"

"Centerville," said Miss Finch in a preoccupied fashion, hand to chin.

"Then this is all the hospital there is, huh?"

"Yes."

"What's the matter with these ginks?" said Doughface nodding his head to right and left.

"That's Tom Johnson," said Miss Finch. "He's dying of cancer and the doctor is going to operate later in the day. And this is Jenny Stevens. She was in an accident last night—poor thing. You had better be very quiet. They're very sick."

"Jake with me," said Doughface. "You mean it about that chicken and ice cream?"

Miss Finch smiled and went out.

Doughface turned over and regarded the man for some time. The fellow was barely conscious and at long last he turned his head.

"How ya feel, pal?" said Doughface.

The man's lips moved but no sound came forth.

"Hard lines," said Doughface sympathetically.

The man moved his lips again and this time he spoke. "Heart's almost gone. But I hope Doc Pellman's gonna fix it. I know I wasn't none too good but . . ."

"He saved my life," said Doughface. "I guess he's a right guy."

"Shore is," said the man, strongly. "He brung my four children into the world. Ain't nobody hereabouts that'll say nothin' agin Doc Pellman."

He stirred restlessly and looked long at Doughface. Slowly he raised himself up on an elbow and further regarded the tramp.

Unexpectedly Tom Johnson said, "You got a cigarette, cap'n?"

"Me? Naw. They was some snipes in me clothes but I don't see nothin' around now."

Johnson raised himself higher and glanced around the room. An ashtray was under the window and he could see the butts in it. He swung down his feet and stretched. He shuffled across the floor and fished out a butt. He found some matches and brought the tray back to Doughface.

Again Johnson stretched and then took a luxurious puff. "Ain't enough air in here," he said, crossing to the window and throwing it open. He stood in the chill blast, again stretching.

"My goodness but I feels good," said Johnson.

Doughface was disappointed a little, but grinning just the same. "Yeah, I put on an act like that plenty of times. What'd you want, some free meals?"

"Ac'?" blinked Johnson. "Say, Doc Pellman was wrong. He said I was gonna die maybe. But I ain't gonna die. I feels like I could lift this buildin' sky-high."

Doughface grinned knowingly. The girl in the other cot stirred a bit and Doughface turned to grin at her. "Whatcha know about that, sister? Tom here pullin' a fake to squeeze a free handout from a right guy like this Pellman."

The girl turned her head painfully to look at Doughface. Her voice was very faint. "What?"

"I said Tom was tryin' to gyp the old man. But what the deuce. I done it myself lots of times. What was you doin'? Neckin' party or one arm drivin' or somethin'?"

The girl stirred. "Drivin'?" Until that moment she had not realized where she was. She started to put her arm down and found that it was in a cast. The weight of bandages on her face was suddenly smothering to her and she pried them away from her mouth and nose.

"How long have I been here?" she queried.

"The nurse said since last night," said Doughface. "She claimed you was on a wild party. . . ."

The girl sat up straight. "I was not! The other man was at fault. He was on the wrong side of the road! Was Bob hurt?"

"Who's Bob?" said Doughface.

The girl looked wildly around her to make sure Bob wasn't there.

Miss Finch came in at that moment with a tray for Doughface—chicken, ice cream and all. She saw Johnson standing by the window in his nightshirt and gave a gasp of horror.

"Get in bed!" cried Miss Finch. "You're due to be operated on in an hour!" She turned and saw the girl sitting up. "For heaven's sake! Lie down! You've got a compound fracture and your face . . . Jenny Stevens! What have you been doing to your bandages?"

The girl pulled at the gauze so that she could see better and Miss Finch stopped dead.

The nurse managed to recover her wits. She advanced on Jenny and moved the gauze again.

"But it can't be!" cried the nurse. "That eye was out! There was an inch splinter of glass in it! But . . . but maybe it was the other eye." She lifted the other bandage and a healthy blue orb blinked at her in a puzzled way. "I must have been mistaken. . . ." said Miss Finch shakily. "But . . . but no. I wasn't! I held your eye open while he took the glass out. He said you couldn't ever see again."

To find out more about *The Tramp* and how you can obtain your copy, go to www.goldenagestories.com.

Glossary

STORIES FROM THE GOLDEN AGE *reflect the words and expressions used in the 1930s and 1940s, adding unique flavor and authenticity to the tales. While a character's speech may often reflect regional origins, it also can convey attitudes common in the day. So that readers can better grasp such cultural and historical terms, uncommon words or expressions of the era, the following glossary has been provided.*

AAA: Agricultural Adjustment Administration; former US government agency established in 1933 under President Franklin Roosevelt. Its purpose was to help farmers by reducing the production of certain common crops, thus raising farm prices and encouraging more diversified farming. Farmers were given benefit payments in return for limiting acreage given to common crops. The agency also oversaw a large-scale destruction of existing crops and livestock in an attempt to reduce surpluses. In 1936, the Supreme Court declared the AAA as unconstitutional.

astern: in a position behind a specified vessel.

Astor: Hotel Astor; located between Forty-fourth and Forty-fifth streets on Broadway, the Astor brought New Yorkers, as well as the world, in droves to what would soon be Times Square. Its design combined a number of different artistic styles and was meant to approximate the luxurious European spas and resorts.

athwartship: across a ship from side to side.

auks: a name given to various species of Arctic sea birds having a chunky body, short wings and webbed feet.

bandoliers: broad belts worn over the shoulder by soldiers and having a number of small loops or pockets, for holding cartridges.

bells: the strokes on a ship's bell, every half-hour, to mark the passage of time.

bitt: a vertical post, usually one of a pair, set on the deck of a ship and used for securing cables, lines for towing, etc.

bolero: a jacket ending above or at the waistline, with or without collar, lapel and sleeves, worn open in front.

bosun: a ship's officer in charge of supervision and maintenance of the ship and its equipment.

bowline on the bight: a bowline knot (a loop knot that neither slips nor jams) with a double loop tied in the bight (middle or slack part) of a rope.

bucko mate: the mate of a sailing ship who drives his crew by the power of his fists.

burg: city or town.

camphor: camphor laurel; a large ornamental evergreen tree, native to Taiwan, Japan and some parts of China. It grows up to seventy feet tall and has leaves with a glossy, waxy appearance.

Cape Town: capital of the Republic of South Africa. A port city founded in the seventeenth century as a stopover for ships plying the Europe-to-India route.

chronometer: an instrument for measuring time accurately in spite of motion or varying conditions.

Confederate: of or pertaining to the Confederate States of America (1861–1865), the government established by eleven Southern states of the US after their secession from the Union. At the onset of the Civil War, the Confederate government issued its own currency which at first was accepted throughout the South as a medium of exchange. The money lost all value when the Confederacy ceased to exist as a political entity at the end of the war.

cracky, by: an exclamation used to express surprise or to emphasize a comment.

dagnab: doggone; an exclamation of disappointment, irritation, frustration, etc.

ensign: a naval flag used to indicate nationality.

fathom: a unit of length equal to six feet (1.83 meters), used in measuring the depth of water.

FLC: Farm Labor Contractor; establishment primarily engaged in supplying labor for agricultural production.

Flying Dutchman: the name of the cursed spectral ship on an endless voyage, trying to round South Africa, the Cape of Good Hope, against strong winds and never succeeding. It has been the most famous of maritime ghost stories for more than 300 years.

fo'c's'le: forecastle; the upper deck of a sailing ship, forward of the foremast.

founder: to sink below the surface of the water.

giddap: alteration of "get up"; used as a command to a horse to start moving.

ginks: fellows.

G-men: government men; agents of the Federal Bureau of Investigation.

goldurned: goddamned; used as an expression of anger, disgust, etc.

gum, by: an exclamation of surprise.

gunwale: the upper edge of the side of a boat. Originally a gunwale was a platform where guns were mounted, and was designed to accommodate the additional stresses imposed by the artillery being used.

halyard: a rope used for raising and lowering a sail.

hard lines: that's tough; something that one says in order to express sympathy for someone.

hawser: a thick rope or cable for mooring or towing a ship.

Hobart: capital and principal port of Tasmania, southeast Australia.

HOLC: Home Owners' Loan Corporation; an agency established in 1933 under President Franklin Roosevelt. Its purpose was to refinance homes to prevent foreclosure (the action of taking property that was bought with borrowed money, because the money was not paid back as formally agreed). The HOLC made about 100 million low-interest loans between June of 1933 and June of 1936.

jake: satisfactory; okay; fine.

keel: a lengthwise structure along the base of a ship, and in some vessels extended downwards as a ridge to increase stability.

largess: money generously bestowed.

lucre: money, wealth or profit.

lying to: stopping with the vessel heading into the wind.

Madeira: a rich, strong white or amber wine, resembling sherry.

marlinespike: a tool made from wood or metal, and used in rope work for tasks such as untwisting rope for splicing or untying knots that tighten up under tension. It is basically a polished cone tapered to a rounded point, usually six to twelve inches long, although sometimes it is longer.

monkey fist: a ball-like knot used as an ornament or as a throwing weight at the end of a line.

newfangled: of the newest style or kind.

Old Glory: a common nickname for the flag of the US, bestowed by William Driver (1803–1886), an early nineteenth-century American sea captain. Given the flag as a gift, he hung it from his ship's mast and hailed it as "Old Glory" when he left harbor for a trip around the world (1831–1832) as commander of a whaling vessel. Old Glory served as the ship's official flag throughout the voyage.

painter: a rope, usually at the bow, for fastening a boat to a ship, stake, etc.

pilot bread: a hard thin unsalted bread or biscuit formerly eaten aboard ships or as military rations.

piqué: a tightly woven fabric with various raised patterns.

poop: poop deck; a deck that constitutes the roof of a cabin built in the aft part of the ship. The name originates from the Latin *puppis,* for the elevated stern deck.

purblind: completely blind.

quarterdeck: the rear part of the upper deck of a ship, usually reserved for officers.

range light: two white lights carried by a steamer to indicate her course.

rapier: a small sword, especially of the eighteenth century, having a narrow blade and used for thrusting.

RFD: Rural Free Delivery; the service by which the United States Postal Service delivers mail directly to residents in rural areas. Prior to its establishment, the residents of rural America had to travel to the nearest post office to get their mail or pay private companies to deliver it.

right guy: good guy.

running light: one of the lights carried by a ship at night and comprising a green light on the starboard side, a red light on the port side, and on a steamer a white light at the foremast head.

Scheherazade: the female narrator of *The Arabian Nights,* who during one thousand and one adventurous nights saved her life by entertaining her husband, the king, with stories.

schooner: a fast sailing ship with at least two masts and with sails set lengthwise.

schooner's house: a structure rising above the deck of a schooner that encloses the bridge.

sea anchor: a device, such as a conical canvas bag, that is thrown overboard and dragged behind a ship to control its speed or heading.

snipes: cigarette butts.

snuffbox: a box for holding snuff, especially one small enough to be carried in the pocket. Snuff is a preparation of tobacco, either powdered and taken into the nostrils by inhalation, or ground and placed between the cheek and gum.

sou'wester: a waterproof hat with a wide brim that widens in the back to protect the neck in stormy weather, worn especially by seamen.

spavined: suffering from, or affected with, a disease of the joint in the hind leg of a horse (corresponding anatomically to the ankle in humans) where the joint is enlarged because of collected fluids.

spring wagon: a light farm wagon equipped with springs.

sprit: a small pole running diagonally from the foot of a mast up to the top corner of a fore-and-aft sail, to support and stretch it.

squaresa'ls: square sails; four-cornered sails suspended from the ship's horizontal yards, long rods mounted crosswise on a mast that support and spread the sails. Square sails are on tall ships, which are called "square riggers."

stern: the rear end of a ship or boat.

t'gal'nts: topgallants; the mast or sail above the mainmast, or mainsail in a square-rigged ship.

thwart: a seat across a boat, especially one used by a rower.

took to his heels: ran away.

truck: vegetables raised for the market.

Vanderbeck: the captain of the ship *The Flying Dutchman*, a ghost ship doomed to forever sail oceans without ever succeeding in rounding the Cape of Good Hope. The legend is said to have started in 1641 when a Dutch ship sank off the coast of the Cape of Good Hope. The ship hit a treacherous rock and as it plunged downwards, Captain Vanderbeck, knowing death was approaching and not ready to die, screamed out a curse: "I *will* round this Cape even if I have to keep sailing until doomsday!" Satan, overhearing his boasting, doomed him for all eternity to precisely that—sailing forever.

windward: facing the wind or on the side facing the wind.

WPA: Works Projects Administration; former US government agency established in 1935 under President Franklin Roosevelt when unemployment was widespread. The goal of the WPA was to employ most of the people on relief on useful projects until the economy recovered. WPA's building program included the construction of 116,000 buildings, 75,000 bridges, 651,000 miles (1,047,000 km) of road and the improvement of 800 airports.

Yankee: a native or inhabitant of one of the northeastern states of the US that sided with the Union in the American Civil War (1861–1865). The *Union* refers to the northern states that remained a part of the United States government during the American Civil War.

L. Ron Hubbard
in the Golden Age
of Pulp Fiction

*In writing an adventure story
a writer has to know that he is adventuring
for a lot of people who cannot.
The writer has to take them here and there
about the globe and show them
excitement and love and realism.
As long as that writer is living the part of an
adventurer when he is hammering
the keys, he is succeeding with his story.*

*Adventuring is a state of mind.
If you adventure through life, you have a
good chance to be a success on paper.*

*Adventure doesn't mean globe-trotting,
exactly, and it doesn't mean great deeds.
Adventuring is like art.
You have to live it to make it real.*

—*L. Ron Hubbard*

L. Ron Hubbard
and American
Pulp Fiction

BORN March 13, 1911, L. Ron Hubbard lived a life at least as expansive as the stories with which he enthralled a hundred million readers through a fifty-year career.

Originally hailing from Tilden, Nebraska, he spent his formative years in a classically rugged Montana, replete with the cowpunchers, lawmen and desperadoes who would later people his Wild West adventures. And lest anyone imagine those adventures were drawn from vicarious experience, he was not only breaking broncs at a tender age, he was also among the few whites ever admitted into Blackfoot society as a bona fide blood brother. While if only to round out an otherwise rough and tumble youth, his mother was that rarity of her time—a thoroughly educated woman—who introduced her son to the classics of Occidental literature even before his seventh birthday.

But as any dedicated L. Ron Hubbard reader will attest, his world extended far beyond Montana. In point of fact, and as the son of a United States naval officer, by the age of eighteen he had traveled over a quarter of a million miles. Included therein were three Pacific crossings to a then still mysterious Asia, where he ran with the likes of Her British Majesty's agent-in-place

L. Ron Hubbard, left, at Congressional Airport, Washington, DC, 1931, with members of George Washington University flying club.

for North China, and the last in the line of Royal Magicians from the court of Kublai Khan. For the record, L. Ron Hubbard was also among the first Westerners to gain admittance to forbidden Tibetan monasteries below Manchuria, and his photographs of China's Great Wall long graced American geography texts.

Upon his return to the United States and a hasty completion of his interrupted high school education, the young Ron Hubbard entered George Washington University. There, as fans of his aerial adventures may have heard, he earned his wings as a pioneering barnstormer at the dawn of American aviation. He also earned a place in free-flight record books for the longest sustained flight above Chicago. Moreover, as a roving reporter for *Sportsman Pilot* (featuring his first professionally penned articles), he further helped inspire a generation of pilots who would take America to world airpower.

Immediately beyond his sophomore year, Ron embarked on the first of his famed ethnological expeditions, initially to then untrammeled Caribbean shores (descriptions of which would later fill a whole series of West Indies mystery-thrillers). That the Puerto Rican interior would also figure into the future of Ron Hubbard stories was likewise no accident. For in addition to cultural studies of the island, a 1932–33

LRH expedition is rightly remembered as conducting the first complete mineralogical survey of a Puerto Rico under United States jurisdiction.

There was many another adventure along this vein: As a lifetime member of the famed Explorers Club, L. Ron Hubbard charted North Pacific waters with the first shipboard radio direction finder, and so pioneered a long-range navigation system universally employed until the late twentieth century. While not to put too fine an edge on it, he also held a rare Master Mariner's license to pilot any vessel, of any tonnage in any ocean.

Yet lest we stray too far afield, there is an LRH note at this juncture in his saga, and it reads in part:

"I started out writing for the pulps, writing the best I knew, writing for every mag on the stands, slanting as well as I could."

To which one might add: His earliest submissions date from the summer of 1934, and included tales drawn from true-to-life Asian adventures, with characters roughly modeled on British/American intelligence operatives he had known in Shanghai. His early Westerns were similarly peppered with details drawn from personal

Capt. L. Ron Hubbard in Ketchikan, Alaska, 1940, on his Alaskan Radio Experimental Expedition, the first of three voyages conducted under the Explorers Club flag.

experience. Although therein lay a first hard lesson from the often cruel world of the pulps. His first Westerns were soundly rejected as lacking the authenticity of a Max Brand yarn (a particularly frustrating comment given L. Ron Hubbard's Westerns came straight from his Montana homeland, while Max Brand was a mediocre New York poet named Frederick Schiller Faust, who turned out implausible six-shooter tales from the terrace of an Italian villa).

Nevertheless, and needless to say, L. Ron Hubbard persevered and soon earned a reputation as among the most publishable names in pulp fiction, with a ninety percent placement rate of first-draft manuscripts. He was also among the most prolific, averaging between seventy and a hundred thousand words a month. Hence the rumors that L. Ron Hubbard had redesigned a typewriter for faster keyboard action and pounded out manuscripts on a continuous roll of butcher paper to save the precious seconds it took to insert a single sheet of paper into manual typewriters of the day.

That all L. Ron Hubbard stories did not run beneath said byline is yet another aspect of pulp fiction lore. That is, as publishers periodically rejected manuscripts from top-drawer authors if only to avoid paying top dollar, L. Ron Hubbard and company just as frequently replied with submissions under various pseudonyms. In Ron's case, the

A MAN OF MANY NAMES

Between 1934 and 1950, L. Ron Hubbard authored more than fifteen million words of fiction in more than two hundred classic publications. To supply his fans and editors with stories across an array of genres and pulp titles, he adopted fifteen pseudonyms in addition to his already renowned L. Ron Hubbard byline.

Winchester Remington Colt
Lt. Jonathan Daly
Capt. Charles Gordon
Capt. L. Ron Hubbard
Bernard Hubbel
Michael Keith
Rene Lafayette
Legionnaire 148
Legionnaire 14830
Ken Martin
Scott Morgan
Lt. Scott Morgan
Kurt von Rachen
Barry Randolph
Capt. Humbert Reynolds

list included: Rene Lafayette, Captain Charles Gordon, Lt. Scott Morgan and the notorious Kurt von Rachen—supposedly on the lam for a murder rap, while hammering out two-fisted prose in Argentina. The point: While L. Ron Hubbard as Ken Martin spun stories of Southeast Asian intrigue, LRH as Barry Randolph authored tales of

L. Ron Hubbard, circa 1930, at the outset of a literary career that would finally span half a century.

romance on the Western range—which, stretching between a dozen genres is how he came to stand among the two hundred elite authors providing close to a million tales through the glory days of American Pulp Fiction.

In evidence of exactly that, by 1936 L. Ron Hubbard was literally leading pulp fiction's elite as president of New York's American Fiction Guild. Members included a veritable pulp hall of fame: Lester "Doc Savage" Dent, Walter "The Shadow" Gibson, and the legendary Dashiell Hammett—to cite but a few.

Also in evidence of just where L. Ron Hubbard stood within his first two years on the American pulp circuit: By the spring of 1937, he was ensconced in Hollywood, adopting a Caribbean thriller for Columbia Pictures, remembered today as *The Secret of Treasure Island*. Comprising fifteen thirty-minute episodes, the L. Ron Hubbard screenplay led to the most profitable matinée serial in Hollywood history. In accord with Hollywood culture, he was thereafter continually called upon

The 1937 Secret of Treasure Island, *a fifteen-episode serial adapted for the screen by L. Ron Hubbard from his novel,* Murder at Pirate Castle.

to rewrite/doctor scripts—most famously for long-time friend and fellow adventurer Clark Gable.

In the interim—and herein lies another distinctive chapter of the L. Ron Hubbard story—he continually worked to open Pulp Kingdom gates to up-and-coming authors. Or, for that matter, anyone who wished to write. It was a fairly unconventional stance, as markets were already thin and competition razor sharp. But the fact remains, it was an L. Ron Hubbard hallmark that he vehemently lobbied on behalf of young authors—regularly supplying instructional articles to trade journals, guest-lecturing to short story classes at George Washington University and Harvard, and even founding his own creative writing competition. It was established in 1940, dubbed the Golden Pen, and guaranteed winners both New York representation and publication in *Argosy*.

But it was John W. Campbell Jr.'s *Astounding Science Fiction* that finally proved the most memorable LRH vehicle. While every fan of L. Ron Hubbard's galactic epics undoubtedly knows the story, it nonetheless bears repeating: By late 1938, the pulp publishing magnate of Street & Smith was determined to revamp *Astounding Science Fiction* for broader readership. In particular, senior editorial director F. Orlin Tremaine called for stories with a stronger *human element*. When acting editor John W. Campbell balked, preferring his spaceship-driven tales, Tremaine enlisted Hubbard. Hubbard, in turn, replied with the genre's first truly *character-driven* works, wherein heroes are pitted not against bug-eyed monsters but the mystery and majesty of deep space itself—and thus was launched the Golden Age of Science Fiction.

The names alone are enough to quicken the pulse of any science fiction aficionado, including LRH friend and protégé, Robert Heinlein, Isaac Asimov, A. E. van Vogt and Ray Bradbury. Moreover, when coupled with LRH stories of fantasy, we further come to what's rightly been described as the foundation of every modern tale of horror: L. Ron Hubbard's immortal *Fear.* It was rightly proclaimed by Stephen King as one of the very few works to genuinely warrant that overworked term "classic"—as in: *"This is a classic tale of creeping, surreal menace and horror. . . . This is one of the really, really good ones."*

L. Ron Hubbard, 1948, among fellow science fiction luminaries at the World Science Fiction Convention in Toronto.

To accommodate the greater body of L. Ron Hubbard fantasies, Street & Smith inaugurated *Unknown*—a classic pulp if there ever was one, and wherein readers were soon thrilling to the likes of *Typewriter in the Sky* and *Slaves of Sleep* of which Frederik Pohl would declare: *"There are bits and pieces from Ron's work that became part of the language in ways that very few other writers managed."*

And, indeed, at J. W. Campbell Jr.'s insistence, Ron was regularly drawing on themes from the Arabian Nights and so introducing readers to a world of genies, jinn, Aladdin and Sinbad—all of which, of course, continue to float through cultural mythology to this day.

At least as influential in terms of post-apocalypse stories was L. Ron Hubbard's 1940 *Final Blackout*. Generally acclaimed as the finest anti-war novel of the decade and among the ten best works of the genre ever authored—here, too, was a tale that would live on in ways few other writers imagined.

Hence, the later Robert Heinlein verdict: "Final Blackout *is as perfect a piece of science fiction as has ever been written.*"

Like many another who both lived and wrote American pulp adventure, the war proved a tragic end to Ron's sojourn in the pulps. He served with distinction in four theaters and was highly decorated for commanding corvettes in the North Pacific. He was also grievously wounded in combat, lost many a close friend and colleague and thus resolved to say farewell to pulp fiction and devote himself to what it had supported these many years—namely, his serious research.

Portland, Oregon, 1943; L. Ron Hubbard, captain of the US Navy subchaser PC 815.

But in no way was the LRH literary saga at an end, for as he wrote some thirty years later, in 1980:

"Recently there came a period when I had little to do. This was novel in a life so crammed with busy years, and I decided to amuse myself by writing a novel that was pure science fiction."

That work was *Battlefield Earth: A Saga of the Year 3000*. It was an immediate *New York Times* bestseller and, in fact, the first international science fiction blockbuster in decades. It was not, however, L. Ron Hubbard's magnum opus, as that distinction is generally reserved for his next and final work: The 1.2 million word *Mission Earth*.

> **Final Blackout**
> *is as perfect a piece of science fiction as has ever been written.*
>
> —Robert Heinlein

How he managed those 1.2 million words in just over twelve months is yet another piece of the L. Ron Hubbard legend. But the fact remains, he did indeed author a ten-volume *dekalogy* that lives in publishing history for the fact that each and every volume of the series was also a *New York Times* bestseller.

Moreover, as subsequent generations discovered L. Ron Hubbard through republished works and novelizations of his screenplays, the mere fact of his name on a cover signaled an international bestseller. . . . Until, to date, sales of his works exceed hundreds of millions, and he otherwise remains among the most enduring and widely read authors in literary history. Although as a final word on the tales of L. Ron Hubbard, perhaps it's enough to simply reiterate what editors told readers in the glory days of American Pulp Fiction:

He writes the way he does, brothers, because he's been there, seen it and done it!

THE STORIES FROM THE GOLDEN AGE

Your ticket to adventure starts here with the Stories from
the Golden Age collection by master storyteller L. Ron Hubbard.
These gripping tales are set in a kaleidoscope of exotic locales and brim
with fascinating characters, including some of the
most vile villains, dangerous dames and brazen heroes
you'll ever get to meet.

The entire collection of over one hundred and fifty stories is being
released in a series of eighty books and audiobooks.
For an up-to-date listing of available titles,
go to www.goldenagestories.com.

AIR ADVENTURE

FAR-FLUNG ADVENTURE

The Adventure of "X"	*Hurricane*
All Frontiers Are Jealous	*The Iron Duke*
The Barbarians	*Machine Gun 21,000*
The Black Sultan	*Medals for Mahoney*
Black Towers to Danger	*Price of a Hat*
The Bold Dare All	*Red Sand*
Buckley Plays a Hunch	*The Sky Devil*
The Cossack	*The Small Boss of Nunaloha*
Destiny's Drum	*The Squad That Never Came Back*
Escape for Three	*Starch and Stripes*
Fifty-Fifty O'Brien	*Tomb of the Ten Thousand Dead*
The Headhunters	*Trick Soldier*
Hell's Legionnaire	*While Bugles Blow!*
He Walked to War	*Yukon Madness*
Hostage to Death	

SEA ADVENTURE

Cargo of Coffins	*The Phantom Patrol*
The Drowned City	*Sea Fangs*
False Cargo	*Submarine*
Grounded	*Twenty Fathoms Down*
Loot of the Shanung	*Under the Black Ensign*
Mister Tidwell, Gunner	

TALES FROM THE ORIENT

The Devil—With Wings　　*Pearl Pirate*
The Falcon Killer　　*The Red Dragon*
Five Mex for a Million　　*Spy Killer*
Golden Hell　　*Tah*
The Green God　　*The Trail of the Red Diamonds*
Hurricane's Roar　　*Wind-Gone-Mad*
Inky Odds　　*Yellow Loot*
Orders Is Orders

MYSTERY

The Blow Torch Murder　　*The Grease Spot*
Brass Keys to Murder　　*Killer Ape*
Calling Squad Cars!　　*Killer's Law*
The Carnival of Death　　*The Mad Dog Murder*
The Chee-Chalker　　*Mouthpiece*
Dead Men Kill　　*Murder Afloat*
The Death Flyer　　*The Slickers*
Flame City　　*They Killed Him Dead*

119

FANTASY

SCIENCE FICTION

WESTERN

121

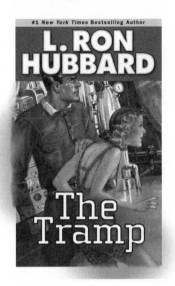